Royston Knapper:
Return of the Rogue

Gervase Phinn is a very proud father of four,
a master of storytelling, a teacher, freelance lecturer, author, poet,
educational consultant and visiting professor of education.

Gervase Phinn's first book of fiction for children,
What's the Matter, Royston Knapper? was published in 2001,
and his first picture book, *Our Cat Cuddles*, in 2002.
Royston Knapper: Return of the Rogue is the second book
in the Royston Knapper series.

Other books by Gervase Phinn

What's the Matter, Royston Knapper?

Our Cat Cuddles

Gervase Phinn

Royston Knapper :
Return of the Rogue

Illustrated by Chris Fisher

For my children:
Richard, Matthew, Dominic and Elizabeth

Published by Child's Play (International) Ltd
Ashworth Road, Bridgemead, Swindon SN5 7YD

www.childs-play.com

Text copyright © Gervase Phinn 2002
Illustrations copyright © A. Twinn 2002
All rights reserved
Printed in Croatia

ISBN 0-85953-024-8 paperback

1 3 5 7 9 10 8 6 4 2

A catalogue reference for this book is available from the British Library

Contents

Going Batty

"It will not have escaped your notice, children," said
Mr Masterson cheerfully, one bright spring Monday morning
in assembly, "that we have a visitor."

All eyes fixed upon the tall stick of a man with shiny
black hair scraped back on his scalp, a pale complexion and
large, dark, piercing eyes. He had long thin fingers like
twigs and protruding teeth.

"This is Mr Dobson, and he's come from the bat
sanctuary to talk to us about the work he does in caring for
these very special little creatures."

"He looks like Count Dracula," said Micky Lincoln
under his breath.

"Good morning, children," intoned the visitor, smiling

widely and displaying an impressive set of white pointy teeth. "I hope that when I have spoken to you about these fascinating and gentle little friends of mine, you will feel the same way as I do. You know, a lot of people don't like bats and are afraid of them."

"I don't like them at all, they're really scary," whispered Fozzy Foster to Royston Knapper.

"I'm not over keen on them either," whispered Royston. "In fact, they give me the creeps."

Mrs Gabbitas did not look too sure either, and screwed up her face as if she was sucking a lemon. Then she gave a little shiver.

"We need to understand and take care of these very unusual and mysterious mammals," continued Mr Dobson. "They are very precious and if we don't look after them they will soon become extinct."

"That's one of the reasons I don't like bats," murmured Fozzy, twisting his mouth into a gruesome scowl.

"Why?" asked Micky Lincoln.

"Because they stink."

"Would you care to share your little *conversazione* with us all, Jamie Foster?" Mr Masterson shouted down the hall.

"Pardon, Sir?" asked Fozzy.

"Your private conversation, your little *tete à tete* with Royston Knapper and Michael Lincoln. Perhaps you might like to tell us all what you were discussing so enthusiastically?"

"It was nothing, Sir," said Fozzy.

"Oh, it was nothing, was it?" laughed the headteacher sarcastically. "You were talking about nothing? How very strange."

"Sir, I was just saying that I don't like bats, Sir," replied Fozzy.

"Well, they probably don't like you," said the headteacher, smiling at his own witticism. "And why do you not like bats, Jamie Foster? Come on, tell us all. I'm sure that Mr Dobson is interested too."

"Because they stink."

"They certainly do not stink!" exclaimed Mr Dobson, with the expression of one who has been grossly insulted.

"You said they did, Mr Dobson," retorted Fozzy blithely.

"I said nothing of the sort," snapped Mr Dobson. "I said that bats are very precious creatures and if we do not look after them, they will soon become extinct, that they would die out. They might very well disappear from the face of the earth if we don't preserve them."

"Don't you think he looks a bit like a bat?" Royston asked Micky under his breath.

"He does a bit," agreed Micky in a whisper.

"Now, does anyone know anything about bats?" asked Mr Dobson, scanning the faces before him.

"I think they're nice," said Penelope Pringle.

"That's because she's batty," said Royston to Rajvir Singh who was sitting in front of him.

"There's bats in the church tower near where I live," continued Penelope, "and they fly round and round. I think they're really cute."

Mr Dobson smiled like a hungry vampire.

"Indeed they are, young lady. They are, in their own way, beautiful, mysterious and fascinating creatures, and we need to respect and protect them. Now, apart from being

nice and cute, what else do you know about bats? What about
you? The young man there. Yes, you." Mr Dobson pointed
to a boy with a face full of freckles and a mop of unruly hair.
"You seemed to have a lot to say to your friend."

It was now Mr Masterson's turn to pull a face.

"They come out at night and bite your neck," said
Royston Knapper enthusiastically. This was followed by a
ripple of laughter from the children.

"That will do!" cried the headteacher.

"Now, that is a popular misconception," said
Mr Dobson. "Bats are indeed nocturnal, but they don't bite
people's necks. In fact they are frightened of humans, like
many creatures."

"Dracula does," announced Fozzy. "He bites people's
necks. He rises from his dusty coffin at dead of night,
changes into a big black bat with sharp teeth, flutters about
for a bit and then attacks people, sucking their blood and
turning them into vampires. I saw this film called 'The
Blood of Dracula'..."

"Thank you, Jamie," interrupted Mr Masterson. "Dracula is not real. He's made up. He's a figment of somebody's wild imagination."

"Bram Stoker," said Mrs Gabbitas.

"I'm sorry, Mrs Gabbitas, did you say something?" asked the headteacher.

"It was Bram Stoker who wrote Dracula, Mr Masterson."

"Was it really? How very interesting." He was clearly none too pleased by the constant interruptions and continued quickly. "Well, there is no such person as Dracula. And I don't know what you were doing watching horror films late at night, Jamie Foster, when you should have been tucked up in bed or reading a book. Now, Mr Dobson has already told us that bats do not bite people's necks and they do not suck blood."

"Well actually," said the visitor, "there is a certain species of bat - the vampire bat - that does feed on blood, but they all live in South America and suck the blood of cattle, other large mammals and birds."

Mrs Gabbitas pulled a face and shivered again.

"Now does anyone know anything else about bats?"

"They get tangled up in your hair," said Noleen Midgely.

"I wouldn't want to get tangled up in *her* hair," said Royston under his breath to Rajvir Singh. "It would be a fate worse than death."

"That's another far-fetched story," announced Mr Dobson. "No, they don't do that either. They are very sensitive and shy creatures, far more frightened of us than we are of them."

"I don't know about that," Mrs Gabbitas murmured to herself.

"Do you know, they've been around for fifty million years, have bats," continued Mr Dobson, "and they make up a fifth of the mammal population world-wide."

"If there's so many bats, Mr Dobson," remarked

Penelope with a puzzled expression on her face, "they can't really become extinct can they? There are just too many of them."

"Now, that is a very interesting observation," said the visitor, nodding vigorously. "You see, some species of bat are more common than others. Some are extremely rare and it is these that we need to protect the most. Did you know that there are nearly a thousand different bat species world-wide? Some are huge with a wingspan of over two metres, but others are tiny and weigh little over a gram. There's blossom bats, butterfly bats, fishermen bats and hairless bats, hammer-headed bats and hog-nosed bats, horseshoe bats and..."

"Vampire bats," added Royston.

"Yes indeed, vampire bats..."

"But they only live in South America," added Royston.

"That's right. Now, some species can live for up to thirty years. Most bats, however, only live for about five years. They are found everywhere in the world, except in the polar regions where it would be far too cold for them. Bats generally like warm climates and hibernate over the cold months. We don't see very much of them because they are very timid and, as I said, only come out at night. Does anyone know anything else about bats?"

"Like my gran's teeth," said Fozzy.

"I beg your pardon?" asked the visitor, frowning.

"My gran's teeth are like bats, they come out at night."

"Don't be silly, Jamie!" snapped Mrs Gabbitas.

"They can fly," said Noleen Midgley.

Her comment was followed by laughter from some of the boys.

"Now that's not such a silly observation," said
Mr Dobson. "Yes indeed, young lady, they can fly and they
are the only mammals that can."

"People can fly," said Fozzy. "I flew to 'Disneyworld'
last summer."

"Jamie," said Mrs Gabbitas. "I will not tell you again.
You went on an aeroplane to 'Disneyworld'. What
Mr Dobson means is that bats are the only mammals with
wings."

"Bats are blind," said Simon Morgan.

"No, bats are not blind, young man," said Mr Dobson,
"in fact they have very good eyesight, especially adapted for
the dark."

"Well, where does 'blind as a bat' come from then?"
asked Fozzy. "My mum's always saying my gran's as blind
as a bat without her glasses."

Mr Dobson was clearly finding this assembly very hard
going. He was used to well-behaved, quiet and attentive
groups of children who listened and paid attention.

"I really don't know where that particular expression
comes from," he replied, getting a trifle agitated by the
constant interruptions, "but it's not true. Now, as I said, bats
are not blind. They have very good eyesight and also use
echolocation to locate their prey. Now before anyone asks,
echolocation is a very high-pitched squeak that the bat
makes, which bounces off objects and lets the bat know if
there is something in its way, or something juicy to eat,"
said Mr Dobson, displaying his impressive set of white teeth
again.

Mrs Gabbitas now looked decidedly uncomfortable and
put her hand to her throat.

"Mr Dobson?" asked Fozzy Foster.

"Yes, what is it now?"

"Could a vampire bat bite a person's neck? I mean, a person's a big mammal."

The visitor sighed.

"Well, I suppose it could..."

"But he would have to be in South America," added Royston.

"Yes, he would," agreed Mr Dobson.

"But it is possible," said Fozzy.

"Yes, but very unlikely."

"But suppose one got smuggled over here," persisted Fozzy.

"I hardly think that could happen," interrupted Mr Masterson. "I can't imagine anyone would want to smuggle a vampire bat into this country." Looking at

Royston, however, he immediately had second thoughts.

"Now the other interesting thing about bats ..." began Mr Dobson.

"Well I read in the paper," announced Fozzy, not dissuaded by the clear irritation which was beginning to show on Mr Dobson's face, "that this woman bought a bunch of bananas from the market, and when she got them home this massive hairy tarantula crawled out and bit her on her hand, and it swelled up as big as a football, and she had to go to hospital, and they had to cut ...."

"We are talking about bats, not spiders!" exclaimed Mr Dobson, who now had two red, angry spots on his pale face. "You certainly have some very inventive and talkative pupils, Mr Masterson," he said, in a tone of voice that indicated he had had quite enough of this interrogation and the frequent interruptions.

"Rather too inventive and talkative at times," replied

the headteacher, giving Fozzy a rattlesnake look.

"Now you are all probably wondering what bats eat," continued the visitor. "Well, there are two types of bat: the fruit-eating bats and the insect-eating bats ..."

"And the ones that suck blood," added Royston.

"Yes, and those that suck blood, but they ...."

"Only live in South America," added Royston.

"Yes, that's right," said Mr Dobson. "There are a few species of bat which eat frogs and toads and fish, and some have been known to eat rats and mice, but they ...."

"Only live in South America," added Royston.

"Yes, that's right," said Mr Dobson.

Mrs Gabbitas pulled a face again and shivered.

"Now bats have little hairy bodies and their wings are made of thin skin, and they have sharp claw-like thumbs to grip onto things."

"It was really gruesome. I couldn't sleep for ages," whispered Fozzy, grimacing.

"What was?" asked Mr Dobson.

"'The Blood of Dracula'. That film I was telling you about."

"Oh dear," sighed Mr Dobson.

"Jamie, if you open your mouth again, you'll be outside my room," warned Mr Masterson. "Now shut up and listen. You might learn something."

"Have you brought any bats in to show us, Mr Dobson?" asked Penelope. "I'd just love to hold a bat. I think they're really cute."

Mrs Gabbitas could not have disagreed more.

"No, I haven't brought any bats in," Mr Dobson told Penelope.

Mrs Gabbitas breathed a sigh of relief. She hated the idea of touching a bat - the fat hairy body like a rat's, the paper skin stretched across the wings, the sharp little hooked claws and the needle sharp teeth. She shuddered at the very thought.

"When we had the man from the owl sanctuary," said Rajvir Singh, "he brought some owls in and let us have them perch on our hands."

"Yes, well owls are not bats!" snapped Mr Dobson. "As I explained to those who were listening, bats are very sensitive and shy, and would be very frightened by all these people. They are also nocturnal creatures, which means that they only come out at night."

"Mr Dobson?" began Noleen Midgley.

"No more questions, please," the visitor spluttered, holding up his hand as if stopping traffic. "I have brought some pictures and bat-file fact-sheets which will answer any other questions you might have. Now, I really must be off. I have another appointment."

Poor Mr Dobson left the school hall very hot and flustered. Never in his life had he experienced such a difficult and demanding audience. How glad he was that he had not gone into teaching. Bats were far easier to handle than children, even vampire bats.

*

"Now don't get any ideas tomorrow," Mrs Gabbitas warned her class. "I have not forgotten last April the First when somebody, and I have an idea who it was, Royston Knapper, placed a large plastic spider on my chair and frightened the living daylights out of me. I do not want a repetition this year, so be warned. No April Fools' Day tricks."

"Miss, why don't you like spiders?" asked Penelope.

"I just don't like them, Penelope," replied
Mrs Gabbitas.

"Don't you like bats either, Miss?' asked Penelope.

"I can't say I share Mr Dobson's obvious enthusiasm
for the creatures," said the teacher. "I'm sure they are very
nice, but I don't like anything creepy and crawly. So, as I
said," she looked in the direction of Royston Knapper, "don't
get any bright ideas tomorrow."

The following morning it was a wary teacher who
approached her desk. She examined her chair. No spider.
She looked in her desk drawer. No spider there either.
She looked under books and behind boxes, but there was no
sign of the creepy crawlies she disliked so much. Soon,

Mrs Gabbitas felt reassured that the children had heeded her warning and she began the lesson.

"Now, Mr Dobson gave us a very interesting insight yesterday into the lives of bats," she told the children. "As I said yesterday, I can't say that I share his liking for them, but they are without doubt, fascinating creatures. What I thought we could do today is write a poem or a description based on what he said, and then mount a display on the walls with some paintings and drawings. Then we could send Mr Dobson some of our work, and of course a letter thanking him for visiting the school. You all have a picture and a copy of the bat-file fact-sheet so there's plenty of information to go on. Remember, nice, neat writing please and use some interesting adjectives and lively verbs."

Soon the children were busily engaged in writing and, as it approached morning break, most had filled a page.

"Penelope, would you like to read your poem or description out, please?" said Mrs Gabbitas.

Penelope took a deep breath and recited her poem in her usual sing-song manner:

> "Cuddly creatures of the night,
> Flying in the moon's pale light,
> Like you, I wish that I could fly
> Up in the tree tops way up high,
> With my little bat-like feet,
> And my little bat-like squeak.
> I'd see the little town below
> And yellow street lamps all aglow,
> The little houses and the station
> Which I do not hit because I have echolocation."

14

"Well, it's certainly different, Penelope," said
Mrs Gabbitas, "but I do wish you wouldn't make all your
poems rhyme."

"I like rhymes, Miss," replied Penelope, rather peeved
by the criticism.

"Yes, I know, dear," said Mrs Gabbitas, "and very good
at rhyming you are too, but there are poems which do not
rhyme and sometimes your rhymes are more important to
you than what you wish to say. The content is more
important than anything else. What about you, Jamie Foster?
Let's hear your effort. You had a great deal to say for
yourself yesterday. I saw you scribbling away like there was
no tomorrow. You have obviously been inspired by
Mr Dobson's talk."

Fozzy took a deep breath and then read loudly and
clearly: "Count Dracula sank his sharp, white, flashing,
pointed teeth into her long, white, swan-like neck.

A fountain of thick, sticky crimson blood gushed and gurgled, spouted and spurted, dribbled and dripped ..."

"Stop right there, Jamie!" commanded Mrs Gabbitas. "That is quite enough. I asked you to write a poem or a description about bats, not a horror story about Count Dracula biting people's necks. You were obviously not listening when Mr Masterson said that Dracula was a figment of the imagination."

"But Dracula was a bat, Miss, a vampire bat," explained Fozzy.

"Which live in South America," added Royston.

"And I have used some interesting adjectives and lively verbs, Miss, like you said we had to," he continued.

"Yes, I know you have Jamie, rather too many, I fear," said Mrs Gabbitas. "But I did not ask for a horror story, did I? What about you Rajvir?"

"What about me, Miss?" asked the boy.

Mrs Gabbitas sighed.

"Could we hear your poem or description, please?"

Rajvir cleared his throat dramatically and read : "On Monday Mr Dobson came into school. He told us all about bats and how we should look after them. He told us they come out at night and there's lots of different kinds. He told us they couldn't harm you. He told us ......"

"Thank you, Rajvir," interrupted Mrs Gabbitas. "Not many interesting adjectives and lively verbs there, I'm afraid." This bat exercise, she thought to herself, had not been such a good idea.

"Miss, can I read mine out?" asked Royston.

The teacher braced herself for another unimpressive piece of writing before replying, "Very well."

Royston took a deep breath and read in a loud, confident voice : "Sometimes, when I'm in the garden at night, I see these little fluttering creatures in the darkness. They look like scraps of black paper blowing in the wind. They only come out at night when all is quiet and still, these shy, harmless creatures. They are called bats. Although I know they are shy, harmless creatures, I still don't like them. I suppose it's their little hairy bodies and their wings made of thin skin and the sharp claw-like thumbs to grip onto things."

"Well, well," said Mrs Gabbitas, smiling widely. "Do you know Royston, that is very good. You seem to have put into words what I feel myself. I'm very pleased with that effort. When you put your mind to it, you can produce some very commendable work."

"Thanks, Miss," said Royston beaming. It wasn't often he received such praise.

It was after morning break when it happened. Mrs Gabbitas went into her storeroom at the back of the classroom to get some paper for the children to copy up their work for the wall display. She emerged holding a small black object, between her finger and thumb.

"I didn't think it would be long before the prankster got up to his old tricks," she said, holding the object aloft. "And who has put this toy bat in my storeroom?"

The children remained silent and just stared.

"If you think I am frightened of a plastic toy bat, you are very much mistaken. Come along, who does it belong to?"

Still there was no answer. The toy had a small furry body, pointed face and a pair of limp, rubbery black wings.

Mrs Gabbitas shook her head and smiled. "Someone hung it on the shelf. The April Fool's over. Whose is it?"

Still no one said a thing.

"Is it yours, Royston Knapper?"

"No, Miss."

"Jamie Foster?"

"No, Miss."

"Michael Lincoln?"

"No, Miss."

"Rajvir Singh?'

"No, Miss."

"Well, it didn't fly in my storeroom by magic," announced the teacher, frowning. "It must belong to someone." She looked in Royston's direction. "Well, if the person who put it there does not own up, I shall deposit this plastic toy bat in the waste paper basket where it will stay."

The class remained silent and still.

Mrs Gabbitas waited a moment before saying, "Right." She headed for the waste paper basket. "In it goes."

Suddenly, the object she held firmly between her finger and thumb twitched and made a tiny squeaking noise. Then, a small bristly head turned and two black pinprick eyes stared up at the teacher.

Mrs Gabbitas froze. Her mouth dropped open and her eyes became wide and glassy. Then she sort of whimpered, "Oh, oh, oh, mmmmmy ggggggooodness mmmmme."

"Christopher Columbus!" exclaimed Royston putting his hands protectively to his throat. "It's a real live bat!"

Fozzy, with a dreadful screeching noise, dived for cover under the desk followed by Simon Morgan. Noleen Midgley, accompanied by several other screaming girls, shot out of the door like rabbits with their tails on fire and Rajvir and Micky Lincoln disappeared into the storeroom.

"Oh, oh, oh, mmmmmy gggggooodness mmmmme," repeated Mrs Gabbitas, rigid with fear, a horror-struck expression on her face.

There was only one person who appeared completely unaffected by the appearance of a real live bat in Mrs Gabbitas' classroom. Quietly, Penelope Pringle stood, walked purposefully up to the near-fainting Mrs Gabbitas, and, taking the trembling creature from the teacher, cupped it gently in her hands and said calmly: "It's all right Miss, it won't hurt you. It's so cute and cuddly. Shall I take it to the school office?"

Mrs Gabbitas, for once in her life, was completely lost for words and merely nodded slowly, up and down, up and down, like one of those fluffy dogs you see in toy shops.

Penelope disappeared out of the classroom door, humming gently to herself. Mrs Gabbitas stood there, silent and speechless, as all the children emerged from the storeroom and from under the desks.

"Well, what do you make of that?' said Fozzy Foster to no-one in particular.

"I've always had my suspicions about Penelope Pringle, you know," remarked Royston Knapper. "They know their own, bats do. I reckon Penelope Pringle could very well be the daughter of Dracula!"

Casualty

"When I woke up this morning, Royston Knapper," began Mr Masterson, in a soft and sarcastic voice, "the birds were singing, the sun was shining and I was really looking forward to a pleasant, and peaceful week ahead. But it was too much to hope for, wasn't it? Too much to expect, that, for just one day, you could keep out of trouble? Quite foolish of me to imagine that I wouldn't see you in front of my desk?"

Mr Masterson paused and sighed.

"And how did it happen this time?" He raised his hand as if stopping traffic. "No, don't tell me. Let me guess. There was an earthquake that caused the books to fall? No? Then was it the ghostly caretaker who had returned to wreak vengeance? Wrong again? Perhaps a little kitten had mysteriously found its way into Mrs Gabbitas's storeroom and caused the accident? Or am I wrong again?"

"Sir," said Royston, in the most innocent of voices, "it just sort of - fell off."

"Ah, it just sort of fell off, did it?" grimaced Mr Masterson. "Well that explains everything, doesn't it? It just sort of – fell off."

"It did, Sir, honest!"

"Like the window last week. Or the fire extinguisher the week before that 'just sort of flew off the wall'. Or what about the time when the tap in the boy's toilets 'just sort of came off in my hand'?"

The tone of the headteacher's voice changed. He leaned over his desk and glowered.

"Do you think I am a complete and utter fool?"

Royston thought it best not to reply to that question. He was in enough trouble as it was.

"Why were you in Mrs Gabbitas's storeroom in the first place?"

"Sir, I was helping Micky Lincoln get a box of books for our reading lesson, Sir. It was right on the very top shelf, sort of balanced, if you see what I mean, and I climbed up to give him a hand with it, and the next thing I knew this massive box of books came down like an avalanche and ended up on top of poor Micky. He was buried in books, Sir, and he had a copy of *Wind in the Willows* sticking out of his mouth."

Mr Masterson breathed out heavily and gripped the edge of his desk.

"Royston Knapper, you attract trouble like a human magnet! Trouble seems to follow you around wherever you

go. Now, I am going to take Michael Lincoln to the hospital, to make sure that he hasn't suffered concussion from the miraculous flying box of books which just 'sort of flew off the top shelf on top of him'. And you, Royston Knapper, are coming with me to keep Michael company. I don't see why I should be inconvenienced waiting in Casualty on a Friday afternoon, while *you* romp off home at four o'clock. Mrs Quinn, the school secretary, will phone your mother and let her know where you are."

"But, Sir ..." began Royston.

"No buts. *You* are coming with me."

The Casualty department at the Royal Infirmary was crowded, noisy and smelly. People with plaster casts on legs and arms; people bruised and bloody on stretchers; people in wheelchairs, on crutches, with sticks; all jostled and queued, and waited for attention.

"Good grief!" exclaimed Mr Masterson. "Just look at this lot. It's like a battlefield. We'll be here until tomorrow morning at this rate."

"Where shall we sit, Sir?" asked Royston, looking around.

"Well, it doesn't look as if there *is* anywhere to sit, it's so crowded. Just take Michael over there, by the doors, and I'll tell them at Reception that we are here. Oh, and don't move!"

As Mr Masterson fought his way through the casualties, Royston led Micky, white-faced and with a large crepe bandage wrapped around his head, over to the doors. He positioned himself next to a sullen-looking boy on the end of a bench. The boy had dusty brown hair resembling an old mop and thick glasses like bottoms of milk bottles, and he looked particularly sad and sorry for himself. He had a large pink plaster on one ear.

"Don't worry, Micky," whispered Royston. "We won't be standing long."

"There's no seats," moaned Micky.

"There will be in a minute," whispered Royston, winking dramatically. Then he began staring fixedly at the boy on the bench.

"Want a picture?" asked the boy, after a while.

"Oh, was I staring?" replied Royston in the sweetest of voices. "I was just thinking how very ill you look."

"Eh?" The boy sat up and took an interest.

"What's wrong with you then?"

"I was bit!" replied the boy, touching the large pink plaster on his ear.

"Lion, was it?"

"Eh?"

"Or a tiger? Mountain lynx? Vampire bat? Grizzly bear?"

"What are you on about?" spluttered the boy. "It was a dog."

"Must have been a pretty big dog to have bitten you up there. Was it a Great Dane?"

"No."

"Old English Sheepdog?"

"No."

"Pyrrenean Mountain Dog?"

"No!" snapped the boy. "If you must know, it was a Chihuahua."

"Chihuahua!" roared Royston.

"I was doing my paper round and it was sitting on this wall. As I passed by, it bit me, on my ear."

Royston could not stop himself from smirking. Even Micky allowed himself a little smile.

"It's not funny," the boy told Royston seriously, still fingering the plaster. "It really, really hurts."

"Well it would do," sympathised Royston. "Very sensitive things, are ears."

The boy brushed a strand of dusty hair from his face and stared over his glasses.

"I only hope they got to you in time," continued Royston.

"What do you mean, got to me in time? In time for what?"

"You know."

"I don't know."

Royston lowered his voice to a conspiratorial whisper.

"To stop you getting rabies, of course."

"Rabies!" the boy exclaimed.

"Very common nowadays, you know, ever since they've dropped quarantine for animals coming over from France."

"I never knew that," murmured the boy, a distraught expression clouding his face.

"Very common nowadays, you know. My dad's a C.O.D. so he should know."

"What's a C.O.D.?" asked the boy, fascinated.

"Catcher of Dogs, of course. He's rounded up lots with rabies. Are you feeling cold by the way?"

"No," said the boy. "Not at all."

"Aye, well," said Royston shaking his head and putting

on a worried expression. "That's the first symptom of rabies, feeling hot and sticky. Then you start burning up and your skin starts to frizzle and shrivel, and you can't swallow properly. Then you start seeing things: flying pink bats and purple slugs, giant hairy spiders and two-headed snakes..."

"Give over!" cried the boy.

"Then your blood starts to bubble and your lungs blow up like balloons, and your eyes pop out and your heart explodes and..."

The boy didn't wait to hear the rest of the grisly account. He was off down the corridor like a frightened rabbit pursued by a terrier, shrieking for his mother.

"Told you we wouldn't have to stand for long, Micky," said Royston cheerfully.

When Mr Masterson found them he was in a terrible mood. He had a large brown stain down the front of his grey suit and was hopping from one foot to the other.

"Did you see that? Did you see that?" he repeated angrily. "An hysterical child ran straight into me and knocked a scalding hot cup of coffee all down the front of my suit!"

"Some people have no consideration," said Royston.

"I shall have to see about getting the stain out. I'll be back in a minute. I see you found a seat." Mr Masterson departed in the direction of the toilets.

Royston now turned his attention to the next person sitting on the bench. This was a large, rosy-cheeked girl with hair in bunches and a leg in an enormous, dirty white plaster cast, which was decorated with an assortment of colourful comments and cartoons.

"Hurt your leg, have you?" asked Royston chirpily.

"No," replied the girl sharply. "I'm waiting for the cross-country to begin."

"How did you do it?" persisted Royston merrily, ignoring her sarcasm.

"Mind your own business," replied the girl. "My mum told me never to talk to strange boys - you never know where they've been."

"Well, I hope they've set it right," said Royston scrutinising the leg. "Looks a bit bent to me, if you don't mind me saying."

"What do you mean, a bit bent?" queried the girl, looking down at her leg.

"Well, sometimes," said Royston in a confidential kind of voice, "they don't set the bones right. My dad works on the buses. One day a conductor on the Number 89 bus, that's the one which goes down Auckley Lane, past the High School and …"

"Oh, get on with it," said the girl.

"Well, this conductor on the Number 89 bus fell down the stairs and broke his leg, just like you."

"Well?"

The girl, despite her aggressive manner, was clearly interested in the account.

Royston lowered his voice to a conspiratorial whisper.

"Well, when they took the plaster cast off, weeks later, his leg was all twisted and bent and gnarled. Looked like the root of an old tree, it did. They had to break his leg again in three places with this big rubber hammer and put another plaster cast on. That conductor didn't punch any more tickets. Then there was my Auntie Christine. Trapped her arm in a door and it snapped like a twig. She had a plaster cast on for weeks and when they took it off, you'll never guess what."

"What?" asked the girl, mesmerised by the gruesome story.

"Gangrene, that's what," said Royston. "Her arm was as green as a cabbage. Then it dropped off. Never played the violin again."

Royston had never seen anybody with a plaster cast move so fast. The distraught girl hopped and hobbled at high speed in search of her father, colliding with a harassed-looking man in a stained grey suit, who had just emerged from the toilets.

"Got a bit more room now, Micky," said Royston, stretching his legs before him. "We can spread out a bit…"

Mr Masterson was in an even worse mood when he returned.

"This place is like a madhouse! First, a stupid boy running into me and spilling scalding hot coffee all down my suit, and then a frantic girl with a great big plaster cast on her leg crushing me against the door of the toilets."
Mr Masterson sighed heavily. "And the day started out so well."

"Sit, down, Sir, and rest your legs," said Royston, getting up from the bench.

"Thank you Royston, but I want to find out how long it will be before the doctor can see Michael," said the headteacher, as he set off in the direction of the reception desk, looking around warily for charging boys, and girls with great plaster casts on their legs.

Royston was just getting comfortable on the bench,

leaning back expansively and resting his head against the wall, when his thoughts were interrupted by a tap on the shoulder. He looked up to see a worried-looking old lady with frizzy hair. She was clutching the hand of a toddler with a chocolate-covered mouth and runny nose.

"Excuse me, love," she said. "Would you mind giving up your seat for an old lady? I can't stand for long, you see, with my bad legs, and I thought to myself, that nice young man won't mind standing for me."

"'Course not," replied Royston half-heartedly, thinking of all the effort and trouble he had gone to.

"Your friend looks proper poorly," the old lady remarked after a while.

"Yes, well he would, wouldn't he?"

"What's the matter with him then?" The old lady shuffled her body into a more comfortable position, the better to hear his reply.

"He's having his stitches out today," said Royston in a matter-of-fact sort of voice. "All forty-eight of them."

"Forty-eight!" The old woman gasped.

"And that's not counting the ones behind his ears."

"Good gracious! Whatever did they do to him?" asked the old woman, staring sympathetically at Micky.

"Brain transplant," said Royston casually. "Got his head caught in a revolving door. Very nasty. Cracked like a nut it was. They managed to fit him with a new brain."

"Well! I've heard of heart transplants and lungs and livers - but never brains!"

"Oh, they're very common these days. I'm thinking of changing mine."

"Go on with you," chuckled the lady. "You must think

I was born yesterday."

"Why are you here?" asked Royston.

"It's my little grandson," said the woman, gesturing to the toddler who was sitting on the bench next to her, swinging his fat little legs backwards and forwards. "Sit still Archie, there's a good boy. He swallowed a marble last week. Doctor gave his mum this thick pink medicine to give him. Said it would work its own way out, you know, down the other end, but we've not seen anything of it so far. I thought I'd bring him to the hospital to be on the safe side."

"You can't be too sure," commented Royston, looking at the remarkably healthy-looking toddler who had now started on another chocolate bar.

"You can't," agreed the old woman.

"My Auntie Moira swallowed a five pence piece once. It was in the Christmas pudding. She nearly choked."

"What happened?"

"They had to cut her open in the end."

"No!"

"Searched for days. Couldn't find it."

"Come on, Archie," said the woman suddenly, snatching the toddler's hand. "We're seeing the doctor right away."

Royston, back on the bench, caught sight of Mr Masterson, striding out in his direction. He looked tired and angry.

"Right!" he said, rushing up to the two boys. "Come along, Michael, the doctor will have a look at your head now. Royston, you remain here. We shouldn't be above five minutes."

The five minutes that Mr Masterson and Micky were away flew by. Royston liked the Casualty department. For a start, he liked the smell of lavender floor polish and disinfectant. Secondly, there were all sorts of interesting people coming and going with an amazing range of injuries: splinters in fingers, nosebleeds, broken limbs, pieces of grit in eyes, burns, dog bites, concussion and nettle stings. He could have stayed there all evening.

In what seemed no time at all Mr Masterson arrived back with Micky, minus the bandage.

"No concussion, I'm pleased to say," he said. "Just a cut and a couple of bruises. So we can be off. I've never been so glad to leave a place. It's like Euston Station at rush hour, people pushing and shouting and screaming and shoving. Do you know, while the doctor was looking at Michael's head, I could hear all sorts of carryings-on in the other cubicles. A shrieking boy convinced he'd got rabies, a stupid girl who kept shouting that her leg was turning green,

and a silly woman wanting a marble removed immediately from a toddler's tummy. I must say, Royston, that compared with that lot, you're a little angel. I don't know how some people get such daft ideas in their heads."

Royston, with a wry smile on his lips, opened the door for Mr Masterson. Then he looked at Micky Lincoln and winked. "I've no idea either, Sir," he said.

Trouble at
Blimpton Gap

Mr Masterson, headteacher of Bogglesview School, would not have looked out of place behind a fruit and vegetable stall at an outdoor market. A large tweed cap, which had seen better days, covered his head; a long brown, woollen scarf was draped round his neck, and thick green corduroy trousers poked out from beneath his old grey raincoat. He would not have sounded out of place behind a fruit and vegetable stall, either, for he had one of those deep, barking voices often possessed by market traders.

Around Mr Masterson, on a cold, wet and windy

afternoon was a knot of pupils with icy hands and bored faces, listening to one of his all-too-familiar monologues. He had been going for a good ten minutes without seeming to draw breath.

"Now, on your right you will see the cliffs - have a look."

Bored faces glanced to the right.

"And on your left you will see the sea - have a look."

Bored faces glanced to the left.

"I do not want anybody up the cliffs or in the sea. Is that clear?"

"Yes, Mr Masterson," chanted the class.

"We are here today on a Geography trip which is an important part of our school work. This is not a seaside excursion and not an excuse for acting the fool. Now look this way."

Fozzy Foster took a small book from his rucksack, flicked through the pages and raised his hand.

"Mr Masterson," he called out.

"Yes, what is it Jamie?"

"Mr Masterson, it says here, in my 'Little Pocket Guide to the Yorkshire Coast' that, 'Blimpton Gap is one of the best examples of coastal scenery in Britain. The high cliffs, rising to over 200 metres in places, have been eroded by the sea for many, many years and are full of caves and caverns.'"

"That's very interesting, I'm sure, Jamie but..."

Fozzy consulted his little book again.

"And, Mr Masterson, it says that this can be a very dangerous coast." He read from the book: 'Especially when it is enveloped by a clinging, cold, damp fog known locally as roak, or sea-fret.'"

"Well, that's all the more reason for us all to be extra careful, isn't it, and ..." started Mr Masterson, but Fozzy continued undeterred.

"And it says in my 'Little Pocket Guide to the Yorkshire Coast', that, 'walking under the cliffs or going in the caves can be extremely hazardous, for apart from falling rock, there is the possibility of ...'"

"Jamie Foster!" snapped Mr Masterson. "This is all fascinating information, but we do need to see the coast and I have a few more words to say before we all disperse. Now put your 'Little Pocket Guide to the Yorkshire Coast' away and listen."

"But, Mr Masterson, it says here..." began Fozzy.

"That will be all, Jamie! We have to get on. Now, everyone has a worksheet, a sharp pencil, a clipboard and a plastic bag in which ..." Mr Masterson paused mid-sentence and his foghorn of a voice echoed off the cliffs : "Timothy Joseph, will you put that down immediately!"

"Sir, I thought we had to pick things up from the beach," replied a little figure in a bright blue anorak and bobble hat.

"Shells, seaweed, fossils, interesting pebbles, but not great big lumps of rotting driftwood with huge rusty nails sticking out of the top!"

"Sir, it could be off a Viking longboat or a Spanish galleon!" cried Royston Knapper, waving his hand wildly in the air.

"Don't be so silly!" snapped Mr Masterson. "Since when did a Viking longboat or a Spanish galleon have 'Produce of Tunisia' written on the side? Now be quiet and listen. I've had just about enough of you already, Royston

Knapper, and we've only just arrived. You've been a nuisance since we set off. Dropping crisp papers on the floor of the coach."

"Yes, Sir."

"Making inane faces out of the window like some mischievous chimpanzee and nearly causing drivers to crash."

"Yes, Sir."

"We'd hardly got out of the school gates and you wanted to go to the toilet!"

"Yes, Sir."

"And stop answering me in that silly tone of voice! Every time I speak to you, you sound like a parrot."

"Yes, Sir."

"You are an irritant, Royston Knapper, a trial and a torment. I suggest that you keep a low profile from now on. Any more out of you, and you will stay with me for the remainder of the afternoon sitting on this large pebble, where I can keep my eye on you!" Mr Masterson gestured towards a round grey rock, half buried in the sand.

Royston wished he had never opened his mouth.

"As I was saying," continued the headteacher. "You all have your worksheet, your pencil and your clipboard and a large plastic bag in which to deposit one or two - I shall say that again - one or two - interesting pebbles, fossils and shells. I do not want half the beach lugged up to the coach and I do not want fish heads, dead crabs, sea urchins and slimy seaweed either. And, Timothy Joseph I hope you are listening, I do not want great big lumps of rotting driftwood with huge rusty nails sticking out of the top!"

Once, Mr Masterson had talked non-stop for a whole hour - sixty minutes of torture. It was like watching an incredibly boring television programme that you couldn't turn off. What was remarkable about Mr Masterson's marathon monologues, quite apart from the length, was that, however exciting the topic, he managed to make it totally uninteresting. He could make the Roman Invasion sound like a visit to the corner shop in heavy drizzle.

Mr Masterson droned on.

"This coast, of course, would be packed with holidaymakers during the summer months, but in November very few people venture down onto the sands ..."

"Mr Masterson," said Fozzy. "It says in my 'Little Pocket Guide to the Yorkshire Coast' that holidaymakers must take care, particularly in the more rocky and secluded places like Blimpton Gap because ..."

"If I hear another mention of that 'Little Pocket Guide to the Yorkshire Coast', Jamie Foster, I shall confiscate it.

41

Now, as I was trying to explain before you rudely interrupted me, very few people venture down onto the sands in this kind of weather."

"I'm not surprised," said Royston Knapper under his breath to Rajvir Singh. "It's cold enough to freeze the flippers off an Arctic penguin down here."

"Who was that?" demanded Mr Masterson. "Who just spoke? Was it you, Royston Knapper?"

Royston put on his angelic expression.

"No, Sir."

"I think it was."

"No, Sir."

"Your mouth moved."

"That was my lips wobbling, Sir."

"And why were your lips wobbling?" asked the headteacher.

"Sir, because I'm cold."

An unpleasant smile spread across the headteacher's face.

"Well, you would be cold wouldn't you?"

"Pardon, Sir?"

"I said you would be cold."

Mr Masterson pointed to a girl dressed like an Arctic explorer.

"Tell us, Penelope, what it said in the letter to parents, about this school trip to Blimpton Gap."

"Sir," replied the girl. "It said we had to be well wrapped-up, Sir, with a thick winter coat or anorak, hat, scarf, gloves, waterproof trousers, sturdy walking boots or wellingtons and ..."

"Thank you, Penelope," said Mr Masterson.

"And are you wearing a thick winter coat or anorak, Royston Knapper?"

"No, Sir."

"What have you got on?" There was a long pause. "Well?"

"My sweatshirt, Sir."

"A sweatshirt. And what about your footwear? Are you wearing sturdy walking boots or wellingtons?"

There was another long pause.

"Well?"

"No, Sir."

"What have you got on?"

"My trainers, Sir."

"Well, is it any surprise then that your lips are wobbling?"

"No, Sir."

"No," grunted Mr Masterson. "Well you will just have to grin and bear it, won't you?"

"Yes, Sir," mumbled Royston, rubbing his hands to get warm.

"Now, Mr McCormack, our coach driver," continued Mr Masterson, "will be picking us up at 2 o'clock on Marine Drive, so we have exactly one hour to explore the beach, looking for one or two colourful pebbles, interesting fossils and different kinds of shells, which we will display when we get back to school. More important, is the completion of the twenty questions on the worksheet and small sketches of the coastal scenery. Now, are there any questions before you depart?"

"Sir, can we go in the caves?" asked Penelope Pringle.

"That's where she belongs," said Royston Knapper to his pal Rajvir Singh. "Prehistoric Pringle, Cavegirl of Blimpton Gap."

"Somebody is talking again!" shouted Mr Masterson.

He turned his attention back to the questioner.

"No, you can't go in the caves, Penelope. Quite apart from the danger, which Jamie Foster has so helpfully pointed out, the caves are used as toilets during the summer months and will be very smelly."

All the class pulled gruesome faces and made strangulated noises.

"EEEEErrrrrrr!"

"Don't be silly!" said the headteacher. "I know, it's not very pleasant, in fact it's rather disgusting, but there's nothing funny about it. So, stay on the beach, well away from the cliffs, the caves and the sea, and remember to be back on Marine Drive for two o'clock for the coach to take

us back to school. And woe betide anyone who is late.
You may go."

The pupils scattered.

Mr Masterson sat on the large grey pebble and,
rummaging inside his capacious rucksack, soon found the
thermos flask he was searching for. He poured himself a
generous cup of coffee in the plastic top, breathed in the
fresh sea air, stared around him at the vast panorama and
decided to have a well-deserved break before he checked on
what the children were doing.

However, five minutes had not elapsed before Penelope
Pringle came galloping across the beach like a frightened
donkey, kicking sand in every direction.

"Sir, Sir!" she cried. "Sir, Royston Knapper's putting
dead crabs down Naseema's boots and, Sir, he threw this big
lump of slimy seaweed in Noleen's face and, Sir, he keeps
skimming pebbles in the sea and splashing everybody and,
Sir…"

"All right! All right, Penelope! That is quite enough! Go and tell that silly boy I want to see him immediately. I have had just about enough of Royston Knapper for one day."

Penelope scuttled off with a self-satisfied expression on her face shouting, "Royston Knapper! Mr Masterson wants to see you!"

She found the culprit behind some glistening black rocks, throwing great big pebbles at a stranded jellyfish.

"Mr Masterson wants to see you, Royston Knapper," she told him. "And you're in deep, deep trouble."

"Ooo-er, I'm dead scared," he replied, putting on a mock-frightened voice.

"Yes, well you will be, because you'll have to sit with him on that big grey pebble for the next hour."

Mr Masterson was only halfway through giving Royston a good telling off, when Rajvir Singh came running at high speed across the sands. He was panting and pointing out to sea.

"Sir! Sir! Come quick!" he shouted.

"Whatever is it, Rajvir?" Mr Masterson snapped, placing the plastic cup full of coffee on the sand and rising from the pebble. "You look as if you've seen a ghost!"

"Sir, come quick! Come on, Sir, quick!"

"Rajvir, what is it?"

"It's an emergency, Sir."

"An emergency?" repeated the headteacher. "What sort of emergency?" He stared nervously up at the cliffs.

"Is someone up the cliffs?"

"No, Sir."

Mr Masterson stared anxiously out to sea.

46

"In the sea?"

"No, Sir."

"Has someone had an accident?"

"No Sir, no Sir."

"Well, what is it, Rajvir? Spit it out!"

"It's Simon Morgan, Sir."

"What about Simon Morgan?" demanded the headteacher, taking hold of Rajvir by the shoulders and looking him full in the face.

"He's stuck."

"Stuck?"

"In a rock."

"In a rock!" repeated Mr Masterson.

"Sir, he's sort of stuck down a crack," spluttered Rajvir, pointing to an outcrop of slimy black, seaweed-covered rocks by the sea's edge.

"Whatever was Simon Morgan doing right out there?" asked Mr Masterson angrily.

"He was looking for colourful pebbles, interesting fossils and different kinds of shells, Sir," Rajvir told him. "And he's got his foot stuck down this big crack."

"Oh, for goodness' sake. Whatever next?" sighed the headteacher. He turned to Royston who was standing on the sand looking innocently out to sea.

"You can come with me," he ordered, stabbing the air with a gloved finger. "Where I can keep an eye on you."

"Yes, Sir," replied Royston cheerily. "But, Sir?"

"What?"

"Could I finish your coffee?"

"Certainly not!"

Grumbling to himself, Mr Masterson strode off purposefully across the clean, grey sand in the direction of the black rocks and the trapped Simon Morgan, followed by Royston, Fozzy and Rajvir. Penelope and Noleen tagged along behind.

When they arrived at the rocks, they found Simon, his face red with exertion, attempting to pull his foot out of a deep narrow cleft. He was moaning pathetically.

"How on earth did you manage to do that, Simon Morgan?" demanded Mr Masterson.

"Sir," the trapped boy sniffed, "Sir, I w...was climbing over the r...r...rocks and I slipped on some s...s...slimy seaweed and my f...foot went whoosh and shot down this c...crack."

"Well, if your foot went in," said Mr Masterson, "it must come out. Give it a good pull."

"I have, Sir," groaned Simon, "but it w...won't budge and it h...h...hurts."

"Oh you silly boy," snapped Mr Masterson, losing patience. "Let me look."

"It's stuck. It won't b...budge," wailed Simon. "I've tried, but it just won't c...come out."

"Have you undone your laces?" asked Royston.

"Yes," whimpered the prisoner in the rock. "But it's made no difference."

"Wiggle it about a bit," Mr Masterson told him.

"Wiggle what about a bit, Sir?" asked Simon pathetically.

"Well I don't mean your bottom, do I?" snapped the headteacher in an exasperated voice. "Your foot, wiggle it about."

"I've w…w…wiggled it but it w…won't move."

"Brace yourself," Mr Masterson told the boy.

"P…p…pardon, Sir?"

"Brace yourself. I'm going to give your leg a short, sharp tug."

"No, Sir," moaned Simon. "No, please, Sir."

"Don't be such a big baby, Simon. You're eleven years old for goodness sake. One short, sharp yank and I'll soon have it out. Now, brace yourself." Gripping his leg firmly the teacher gave a mighty heave.

"Aaaaaaaahhhhhh!" shrieked the boy. "Stop it, Sir! Stop it! It hurts!"

Mr Masterson was now angry, red in the face and flustered.

"As if I haven't got enough to worry about, Simon Morgan," he said, glowering at Royston Knapper.

"Sir," said Royston, "my dad says that in an emergency, it's best not to panic, Sir. My dad says you ought to keep calm and collected, and decide on a clear plan of action."

Mr Masterson suppressed his fury and, with tight lips, turned in the direction of Royston.

"I am not interested in what your father has to say, Royston Knapper, or anybody else for that matter. Kindly keep your clever comments to yourself."

He turned back to the captive in the crack.

"Now, Simon, try again."

"Sir, I c...c...can't, it hurts." The boy's eyes filled with tears and his bottom lip began to tremble. "Sir, I might never get out. I might be stuck here for ever and ever."

"Don't be so silly, Simon." Mr Masterson put his arm around the boy's shoulder and his voice took on a much gentler and more sympathetic tone. "We'll have your foot free in no time. If I can't get it out, then Mr McCormack will be here in less than an hour and he'll soon release you. He'll have all sorts of tools in his coach."

"Yes, Sir," whimpered Simon.

"Now would you like a hot drink to warm you up?" asked the headteacher, reaching for his rucksack.

"Yes please, Sir," whimpered Simon, wiping his streaming nose on the back of his hand.

"A nice strong cup of steaming coffee will make you

feel a whole lot better," Mr Masterson told him, producing the thermos flask.

"I don't like coffee, Sir," said Simon. "Could I have a cup of tea?"

"No," said Mr Masterson sharply. "I only have coffee."

"I'll have a cup, Sir," said Royston cheerfully. "I love coffee."

"No you will not!" exclaimed the headteacher. "You will stay where you are and keep your mouth closed."

Simon sniffed noisily and wiped his nose again, this time on his sleeve.

Mr Masterson pushed a tissue into his hands.

"Give your nose a really good blow," he told him.

Simon made a noise like a distant train.

"I recall when I was a little lad, you know, and I got my head stuck in the railings at the park. I thought I'd never get out, but the fire brigade came and I was free in no time."

51

"More's the pity," remarked Royston to Rajvir Singh.

"What was that, Royston Knapper?" asked the headteacher, swivelling around.

"I said what a pity, Sir. You getting your head stuck."

"Then there was the time," continued the headteacher, "when my son, Roger, was a little boy, and got his toe stuck up the bath tap. He was very frightened at the time, but we all laughed about it later."

"Sir, did he get his toe out?" asked Royston.

"Well, of course he got it out! You don't think he goes through life with a tap on his toe, do you?"

"But I've not got my toe stuck up a tap," groaned Simon. "I've got my foot stuck in a rock."

"I know you've got your foot stuck in a rock, Simon," sighed Mr Masterson. "I can see you've got your foot stuck in a rock. You have told me a number of times you've got your foot stuck in a rock. What I'm saying, is that if I or Mr McCormack can't get you out, we will send for the fire brigade and they will free you." Mr Masterson looked at his watch. "In about forty minutes Mr McCormack will be here, so we will just have to be patient."

"Sir, it'll be too late," said Fozzy.

"What do you mean, it will be too late?" asked the headteacher.

"Sir, the tide's coming in. In my 'Little Pocket Guide to the Yorkshire Coast', under the section –'A Cautionary Note' - it says that there is a possibility of being cut off by the tide, which must be treated seriously. I did try to tell you before, Sir. It says it is all too easy to be caught unawares. Blimpton Gap is famous for its fast rising tides. In my 'Little Pocket Guide to the Yorkshire Coast' it gives the times of the tides and it's high tide here in about an hour."

Mr Masterson's mouth dropped open and his eyes looked large and glassy. He looked out across the grey, oily sea.

"Sir, while we've been talking," said Royston nervously, "all the rock pools have been filling up."

"I'm frightened, Sir," whispered Simon.

For once in his life Mr Masterson was silent, completely lost for words. Through his mind rushed the most terrifying thought of the cold North Sea rushing relentlessly across the beach, rattling the pebbles, sweeping over the rocks and swallowing up the trapped child.

"Sir," pestered Royston. "I could cut the bottom off my lemonade bottle so that Simon could use it as a kind of breathing tube when the sea goes over his head."

There came a strangled cry from Simon.

"Royston," Mr Masterson spoke through gritted teeth. "Will you be quiet? There's no question of the sea going over Simon's head. We'll soon have him out of there. Now you and Rajvir make yourself useful. Run up to the road and stop the first car you see. Tell the driver to get help."

"How, Sir?" asked Royston.

"Well, I don't mean jump out in front of it, do I? Wave the car down and ask the driver to go and get help. Well, go on!"

The two boys scurried off.

"And be careful!" he shouted after them.

"Penelope," Mr Masterson continued. "You and Noleen go up to the telephone kiosk on Marine Drive. You can see it from here. Phone the police and tell them what's happened, and tell them it's not a prank."

The two girls ran off chattering excitedly.

"Naseema."

"Yes, Sir?"

"You and Gillian run over to those two cottages on the edge of the beach. Tell the people living there to phone the police and fire brigade. And we might need the coastguard, the ambulance and air-sea rescue as well. Now hurry."

Mr Masterson, whose face was flushed and hot, turned to Simon. He tried to put on a cheerful voice.

"Now, we'll soon have you out."

"Sir, there'll be a lot of people coming to help," observed Fozzy Foster.

"The more the merrier," said Mr Masterson, staring out to sea.

After what seemed like hours, Penelope and Noleen could be seen running across the sands.

"At last," sighed Mr Masterson looking at the sea lapping at his feet. "Penelope and Noleen are back. The fire brigade will soon be here."

But when he heard the girls' story, his face turned white.

"Sir!" Penelope panted. "Sir, the phone's been pulled out. The kiosk's been vandalised."

"Didn't you get through to the police?" asked the headteacher in a desperate voice.

"No, Sir."

Simon began to sniffle and whimper.

"Never mind, here comes Naseema. She'll have got help."

But when Mr Masterson heard her story he felt quite faint.

"Sir, the cottages were all locked up," Naseema told

him weakly. "They're holiday homes and there was nobody in."

Mr Masterson looked out to sea. Cold grey waves were rushing across the limestone pavement, sweeping up the beach, filling the rock pools and swirling around the pebbles. Great swathes of weed were fanning out beneath the waves, small crabs were emerging from cracks and tiny fish, like slivers of bright glass, were darting beneath the water. The tide was coming in at an alarming rate.

"Sir," Simon whispered in a hoarse voice. "The water's over my ankles."

Two figures could be seen running across the sands.

"Oh no," sighed Mr Masterson. "It's Royston and Rajvir, and there's no-one with them."

The sea was now swirling around Simon's knees and tipping him off balance. He was quiet, white, and trembling. The rest of the children watched anxiously from the sand. Mr Masterson, with water now over his boots, gripped Simon's hand tightly and prayed. Royston scrambled over the slippery rocks towards them, his voice ringing loudly.

"Sir! Sir!" he cried. "Nobody would stop! They thought we were messing about. They wouldn't stop!"

"Stay on the sand!" ordered Mr Masterson. "Don't come any closer."

But the headteacher's voice was carried out to sea on the cold wind and Royston could not make out what he was shouting. Like a monkey, he clambered quickly over the seaweed-covered rocks. Then, as he reached the two figures, knee-deep in water, Royston slipped. His legs shot from under him and his arms waved wildly in the air. He fell forwards, directly onto Mr Masterson, who, losing his

balance, crashed backwards onto Simon. With a great
'Kerplosh' they both disappeared beneath the waves.
Mr Masterson emerged a moment later, like some great
marine creature spluttering, gasping, snorting and spitting
water. He scrambled to his feet shrieking, "You stupid,
stupid boy! Just wait till I get you back to school!"

At that moment, there was a shout from behind him that
echoed off the cliffs.

"I'm free! I'm free!" screamed Simon, splashing wildly
in the water. "My foot, it's come out…it's out…it's come
out! Sir, when you fell on top of me you knocked my foot
out. I'm free! I'm free!"

There was a loud cheer from the children on the beach.
Everyone jumped up and down madly, clapping and
cheering, screaming and shrieking.

Royston had saved the day.

A wet, bedraggled and silent Mr Masterson waited with the children for the arrival of the coach. His large tweed cap had been swept out to sea, his long brown, woollen scarf dangled dripping from his neck, his thick corduroy trousers and his old grey raincoat were shapeless and sodden. He stared vacantly at the grey sea, now crashing against the granite blocks bordering the road. Never in his life had he experienced such sheer terror, such helplessness. Never in his life had he been so silent.

The coach drew up and Mr McCormack popped his round, red face out of the window.

"All aboard for the trip home!" he shouted in a cheerful voice.

The excited children clambered aboard the coach.

Mr Masterson, tight-lipped and without a word, squelched up the steps leaving small puddles in his wake.

"Now then, Mister Masterson," Mr McCormack beamed at him. "Have we had a good time, have we?"

Mr Masterson, with a look that would curdle milk, swivelled round to face him.

"No, we certainly did not have a good time! We had a disastrous time, an appalling time, a horrifying time. We had the worst time I have ever had in my entire life. Now will you kindly get moving. The sooner we are home the better!"

Mr McCormack's mouth dropped open.

"Crikey. What did I say?"

He turned to a cheeky-faced boy with straw-like hair, who was sitting on the front seat.

"I don't know," he said, scratching his head. "Every time I open my mouth these days I seem to put my foot in it."

"It wasn't you who put your foot in it,
Mr McCormack," replied Royston Knapper, attempting to
stop himself bursting into hysterical laughter. "It was Simon
Morgan."

"Eh?" asked the puzzled driver.

"Never mind," said Royston. "It's a long story."

Teachers are Funny Onions

It was Friday afternoon, and Mr Masterson was really looking forward to two quiet, relaxed, uneventful days away from the school. He sighed with pleasure at the mere thought of it. His week had been dreadful. On Monday, the boiler had shuddered and spluttered and then belched out some black, evil-smelling smoke, before seizing up and leaving the school icy cold. When he arrived on Tuesday, he had found puddles in the corridor, walls running with water and a leaking roof. On Wednesday, the dinner ladies had informed him that they were not used to working in Arctic, underwater conditions and promptly left. Thursday, the caretaker had fallen from his ladder on the wet floor and it had taken half an hour, a damp flannel and two cups of very strong sweet tea to revive him. And Friday brought with it a letter from Mr Craddock, one of Her Majesty's Inspectors of Schools, giving Mr Masterson short notice of another impending visit. All in all, the week had been memorable for the number of disasters it had brought.

It was now Friday afternoon. Nothing else could possibly go wrong. The last bell of the week had rung, the children and staff were making their way home, the cleaners were busy in the classrooms, the caretaker was locking the doors and Mr Masterson was tidying his desk before disappearing for his idyllic weekend away from it all in his caravan at Whitby.

There was a faint knock on the door.

"Come in," Mr Masterson shouted cheerfully, but the smile on his face withered as he saw who had entered the room and was standing before him.

"Oh, it's you, Royston," said the headteacher.

"Yes, Sir," replied the boy quietly.

"What is it?'

Royston kept his head down and examined the scuff marks on his shoes.

"You're not in trouble again are you?"

"Well ..." began Royston.

Mr Masterson gripped the edge of his desk to steady himself. No, Knapper can't be in yet more trouble, he thought. Not on Friday afternoon. Not when he was looking forward to his idyllic weekend away from it all in his caravan at Whitby.

"Come on speak up, Royston," he said in a deeply sinister, whispery sort of voice. "What is it you want? Why are you here?"

"Mrs Longbottom sent me in, Sir."

"And who is Mrs Longbottom?" asked the headteacher, attempting to stay calm.

"Sir, she's the lollipop lady, Sir. She stops traffic so people can cross the road."

"I know what a lollipop lady is, thank you very much, Royston. Why has she sent you to me?"

"Well, Sir..." Royston took a deep breath. "It's like this. I was helping Mrs Longbottom at the school crossing and I saw this little old lady by the side of the road, so I started to help her across. It was only when we were in the middle that I realised that she didn't want to cross the road at all. In fact, she was going in the opposite direction.

Anyway, she got really angry with me and started shouting and waving this great big walking stick in the air…"

"Dear-oh-dear," sighed Mr Masterson, slumping into his chair and putting his head in his hands. He began to see his idyllic weekend fading into the distance.

"Anyway, by this time Mrs Longbottom came over to see what all the noise was about and she asked me to hold her lollipop. It's not really a lollipop, Sir, it's a sort of red and yellow sign with 'STOP' on it and when she holds it up…"

"For goodness' sake get on with it!" roared Mr Masterson, gripping the edge of his desk so hard that his knuckles went white.

"Well, Sir, this little old lady turned quite nasty, so I put the lollipop down by the side of the road to help Mrs Longbottom, when it happened."

"When what happened?"

"Sir, this van – it was a bread van actually, 'Golden Glow Bakery' I think…"

"I am not the slightest bit interested in what bakery the van was from," the headteacher told him, trying to stay calm. "What happened?"

"It ran over the lollipop - the van from the 'Golden Glow Bakery' that is - and crushed it."

Mr Masterson's mouth dropped open. Royston thought how like a big fish he looked, with his popping eyes and gaping mouth.

"And that's when the crash happened, Sir."

"Crash! What crash?" repeated Mr Masterson in a hoarse whisper.

"The bread van, when it crushed the lollipop, sort of

screeched and skidded and scrunched to a stop, and this car
ran into the back of it. And that's when the wall got knocked
down."

"Wall? Wall?" repeated Mr Masterson. "What wall?"

"The school wall, Sir. The car, behind the car that went
into the back of the bread van, that went over
Mrs Longbottom's lollipop, swerved to miss the car in front
and it sort of hit the school wall. And that's when Penelope
Pringle got hurt, Sir."

Mr Masterson was lost for words. All he could do was
stare in complete amazement. His tranquil, uneventful
weekend was forgotten.

"You see, Sir, Penelope Pringle was sitting on the wall
when it got knocked over. I think she's more shocked than
anything, but a few stray bricks might have hit her."

"Stray bricks..." Mr Masterson's voice was faint.

"Then the window got smashed."

"Window?" Mr Masterson's voice was barely a whisper.

"When the car hit the wall, it came as such a shock to Penelope Pringle that she threw her satchel in the air and it ended up going through Mr Ahmed's shop window. And that's when…"

"STOP! STOP!" bellowed the headteacher. "I don't want to hear any more!"

There was a thundering knock on the door and what sounded like a lynch mob in the corridor outside.

"That'll be Mrs Longbottom now, Sir," explained Royston, "with Penelope Pringle's mum and the drivers of the cars."

Mr Masterson managed to calm down the posse demanding Royston's blood, but it took all his powers of persuasion and argument. As he climbed into his car at six o'clock, his weekend ruined, he asked himself 'Why?'. Why had fate destined that Royston Knapper, the noisiest, naughtiest, nosiest boy in the world, should attend his school?

On Monday morning, everybody was talking about Friday afternoon.

"It was horrible, really, really horrible," Fozzy Foster was telling a knot of pupils in the school yard. "The lollipop lady, Mrs Longbottom, lives next door to my grandma and she was telling her it was like a scene from a disaster movie - bodies all over the place, cars smashed into each other, buildings demolished, broken glass like confetti, blood running down the gutters and people screaming and shouting and shrieking. I wish I'd been there."

"It was nothing like that," said Royston who had wandered over and joined the group.

"Mrs Longbottom told my grandma," continued Fozzy, ignoring the interruption, "that there was hundreds of pounds worth of damage, and that you were responsible 'cause you were poking your nose into other people's business."

"Well, thank you very much, Fozzy. You're supposed to be a mate."

"I'm only telling you what happened. You have to admit you're never out of trouble. This time you have really gone and done it."

"It'll all have been forgotten by now," remarked Royston hopefully.

But the incident was far from forgotten. In fact, the whole of the Monday morning school assembly, another marathon monologue from Mr Masterson, was devoted to it. Royston thought the headteacher wasn't going to mention what had happened, but then he heard him say:

"I'm going to start this morning's assembly with a poem which has a message for all of us." He fixed Royston, who was on the front row, with his cold, fishy eyes. "And especially for one person present."

Royston wished the floor would open up and swallow him.

In a loud, dramatic voice Mr Masterson began to read :

Sidney Snoop was a nosy child
Who all around him, drove quite wild,
By peering, poking, peeping, prying,
Probing, watching, meddling, spying.

For everything he had to know.
What is that? Where's so and so?
Why and how and when and where?
He always had to stop and stare.

He'd set off early for school each day,
To look in windows on the way.
Into skylights, over ledges,
Under fences, over hedges.

With open mouth and eagle eye,
Sidney Snoop just had to spy.
Peering, poking, peeping, prying,
Probing, watching, meddling, spying.

To miss a thing he couldn't bear
And if he did, he'd tear his hair,
And stamp his feet and bawl and cry.
For Sidney Snoop just had to spy.

With every line, Royston felt sicker and sicker. He could feel everybody's eyes fixed on him, especially Penelope Pringle's. She had come to school in so many bandages, she looked like an Egyptian Mummy. She had told her friends as she limped into school that her mother was on the 'phone to Mr Masterson for an hour at the weekend, complaining about Royston Knapper.

"And that's what can happen to busy-bodies, people who cannot mind their own business," remarked Mr Masterson. Then he did his imitation of a vampire and a thin-lipped, sarcastic smile spread across his face. "Of course we have our own Sidney Snoop in this school, our very own Nosy Parker who meddles in things which don't concern him."

The whole ghastly incident was related in the greatest detail. Royston felt awful and really embarrassed.

But that wasn't the end of it. When he arrived at his classroom, Mrs Gabbitas, his teacher, had to have her say.

"You were very lucky, Royston, that things were not a whole lot worse."

"What about me, Miss?" interrupted Penelope Pringle indignantly.

"I realise you had a nasty shock, Penelope, but what I mean is someone could have got seriously injured, perhaps killed." Mrs Gabbitas stared at Royston and shook her head. "I hope you've learnt your lesson."

"Yes, Miss."

"When I looked out of this window on Friday afternoon, I couldn't believe my eyes. It looked as if a tornado had hit the street."

"Miss, we don't get tornadoes in England," said Fozzy. "'In my 'Little Pocket Guide to the Weather' it says…"

"Thank you, Jamie Foster. I am fully aware of that. What I meant was it looked as if all the damage had been caused by a dangerous and destructive wind like a tornado."

"Miss, I was only trying to help…" Royston began.

"Help!" said Mrs Gabbitas, giving a hollow laugh. "Is that what you call it?"

"Yes, Miss."

"Well all I can say, Royston, is that when you 'help' somebody, it is always followed by a catastrophe. 'I was only wanting to stroke the gerbil because he looked lonely': then it escapes and causes havoc. 'I was only looking to see if the caretaker had fixed the new light bulb': then he gets knocked off his ladder. 'I was only helping a little old lady cross the road', a road which in fact she didn't want to cross in the first place: then we have a re-run of the Second World

War! I would suggest, Royston, that in future you don't
'help'. Mind your own business and keep your nose out,
because one of these days, if you don't, you might just get it
bitten off. Now there's an end to the matter. Let's get on
with our work."

But it was not the end of the matter by any means. Just
before morning break Mrs Quinn, the school secretary,
arrived at the classroom.

"Royston Knapper's to come to the headteacher's room
immediately," she announced primly. "Mr Masterson wants
to see him." Then she added, "And there's a policeman with
him."

Royston's heart sank. He followed Mrs Quinn as she
waddled down the corridor ahead of him, his heart banging
away in his chest and his face hot and sticky. As Royston
entered the headmaster's office, Mr Masterson was standing
by the window, hands clasped behind his back, looking over
the school fields. Next to him was a big hairy policeman.

"Come right in!" snapped Mr Masterson. He turned to the policeman. "This is the boy, Constable Hardcastle, the silly lad who caused all the damage on Friday."

The policeman stared at Royston for a moment, stuck out his chin, sniffed and coughed.

"Now then, young man," he began. "I've got a few well-chosen words to say to you."

"What did that policeman want?" asked Micky Lincoln at morning break.

"He told me off," said Royston. "He said I ought to stop poking my nose in things that don't concern me, and that people could have got hurt. He said the next time I see him, it'll be to arrest me and lock me away in a prison where I can't get up to any mischief. And he said he's going to have a word with my dad. And he says he's going to keep an eye out for me from now on. All I was doing was trying to help a little old woman cross the road. That's all the thanks you get for trying to be helpful."

For the rest of the day Royston was unusually quiet. The caretaker intercepted him on his way into the dinner hall and told him he was a very silly and meddlesome boy. He pointed at him with a long plaster-covered finger, the one the gerbil had bitten. Mrs Crabtree, senior dinner lady, wrapped up in a large, duvet-like coat in case the boiler broke down again, slopped the meat pie and shovelled the chips onto Royston's plate at lunchtime, and grunted: "Stupid boy!" At four o'clock on his way home, Royston was spotted by Mrs Longbottom who gave him a withering look and shook a crumpled lollipop sign at him.

By Friday of that week, things were beginning to return to normal. Apart from the odd comment from Penelope, nobody mentioned what had happened the week before. It was just before afternoon break that Mrs Quinn arrived, summoning Royston to the headteacher's room again.

"And this time there's a police inspector and a sergeant with him," she announced, almost gleefully.

Royston must have looked terrified, for Mrs Gabbitas put a friendly hand on his shoulder and smiled reassuringly.

"Don't get all worried, Royston. I'm sure it's nothing serious. They stopped chopping people's heads off and locking them in deep, dark, smelly dungeons years ago."

"More's the pity," mumbled Mrs Quinn, screwing up her face as she waddled for the door.

Following the dumpy figure of Mrs Quinn down the school corridor that led to Mr Masterson's room, Royston knew what the American gangsters on Death Row must have felt like on their journey to the Electric Chair, or what the aristocrats at the time of The French Revolution felt like on their way to the guillotine. He felt wobbly with fear and had a sort of cold, empty feeling in the pit of his stomach. A police inspector, he thought. He's come to take me away!

"He's probably come to take you away," remarked Mrs Quinn without turning around. "Causing all that trouble and damage. Probably going to lock you up in one of those places where they put naughty boys."

Royston was not expecting the reception he received when he was shown into the headteacher's room. As soon as he set foot through the door, a tall, thin police inspector, with fluffy little outcrops of white hair like cotton wool, small grey eyes and a silly, wide smile across his face, came

72

forward to greet him.

"Well, well, well," the policeman repeated, his smile spreading even wider. "You must be very proud of this little chap, Mr Masterson. Very proud indeed."

Proud? thought Royston, stunned. Is he being sarcastic?

"If more young people acted as he has done, showing concern for others, displaying initiative and common sense and public spirit, we'd live in a much better world. You hear so much these days about hooligans and teenage vandals, and children running wild. It's nice to know there are still youngsters like Royston here to set an example of behaviour to others."

Royston wondered if this were a dream. Concern for others? Initiative? Common sense? Public spirit? What was the man on about? Was he mad?

"Yes, indeed," mumbled Mr Masterson, his voice distinctly unenthusiastic. "Most commendable."

It must be catching, thought Royston. Now the headteacher's gone mad!

"I was just saying to Sergeant Snaith here," continued the inspector, nodding in the direction of his mountainous colleague behind him, "that if you hadn't used your common sense and acted as quickly as you did, Mr Gomersall might not be alive today to tell the story."

Oh! thought Royston. Mr Gomersall! They weren't talking about the crash at the school crossing. It was old Mr Gomersall they were talking about.

Royston had first met Mr Gomersall two years before, when he had delivered a parcel after the school's Harvest Festival. Most of the food had been eaten by Royston on the way to the old man's house, but Mr Gomersall had not seemed to mind and was pleased to have somebody to talk to. Royston liked the old man from the start. He wasn't like some old people: always moaning and groaning about their ailments, complaining about the state of the country and the behaviour of children, grumpy and bad-tempered and moody. Mr Gomersall was as chirpy and lively as a canary. He told jokes, wore jeans and an old baseball cap, liked pop music and had tattoos on his arms, and sometimes he swore and chewed thick black tobacco which made him look as if he had a mouthful of motor oil. Mr Gomersall was more like a friend than anything.

Every morning on his way to school, Royston passed Mr Gomersall's old, red-brick, terraced house on Canal Road. The old man was always at the window, looking at passers-by, and watching the barges and boats chugging noisily up and down the canal. Royston gave the old man a thumbs-up sign and Mr Gomersall waved back.

One morning, the week before the incident at the school crossing, there had been no sign of Mr Gomersall. Royston had peered through the front room window, but the inside was dark. He hadn't seen anything through the back kitchen window either, nor through the letter-box. At first his knocks had been light, but when there was no response, Royston had started banging very hard on the kitchen door. The great thundering bangs had started Buster off barking and brought the next-door neighbour out. The neighbour was a fat man wearing a grubby vest and an enormous leather belt.

"What's going on?" he had demanded.

"It's Mr Gomersall, he's not answering his door," Royston had explained.

"He's probably not up yet," the man had said, turning to go back inside his house.

"He's always up at this time."

"Well, he's not today, so clear off!" the man had said,

yawning like a sleepy hippopotamus.

Royston had returned to hammering on the door.

"Mr Gomersall! Mr Gomersall! Are you all right?"

"If you don't clear off," the neighbour had shouted, "I'll give you a clip round the ear!"

"You can do what you want," Royston had retorted. "I'm not going anywhere until I see Mr Gomersall." Then he started banging on the door again.

The neighbour had taken some persuading, but eventually agreed to force open the kitchen door. They had found the old man stretched out at the foot of the stairs where he had fallen. Buster was standing by his feet, grunting and growling. Mr Gomersall had looked grey and very old, but he was still breathing slightly. While the neighbour had telephoned for an ambulance, Royston had covered the old man with a blanket and put a cushion under his head. Help hadn't been long in arriving, and when Royston had seen the ambulance disappear around the corner of Canal Road, sirens blaring and blue lights flashing, he had carried on with his journey to school.

Royston had called in at the hospital on his way home that afternoon and found Mr Gomersall propped up in bed as cheerful and chirpy as ever, and very grateful for what Royston had done. A cheerful-looking nurse with red cheeks had said how sensible and how kind Royston had been, and even the doctor commented on his 'good deed'.

"Yes indeed," the police inspector was saying now. "You very probably saved the old man's life." He turned to the headteacher. "You should be very proud of this young man, very proud indeed."

Mr Masterson gave a weak smile.

On Monday morning, the headteacher devoted the whole school assembly to the theme of helping others. He read the part in the Bible about 'The Good Samaritan', who helped the man who had been robbed.

"Of course, we have our own 'Good Samaritan' in this school, who acted sensibly, swiftly and selflessly, and almost certainly saved an old man's life."

Then the whole story of how Royston had helped Mr Gomersall was related in the greatest detail.

"You know," said Fozzy Foster at morning break, to the knot of pupils in the school yard. "Teachers are funny onions. One minute they tell you to mind your own business, to keep your nose out, and not to meddle in things that don't concern you, and the next minute they're telling you to do the very opposite."

"I don't know about that," said Micky Lincoln, "but I

know one thing for sure. If Royston Knapper fell in the biggest, smelliest, squelchiest pile of manure, he'd come out smelling of roses."

The Football Match

It was the final junior assembly of the week and
Mr Draycott, the deputy headmaster of Bogglesview School,
looked far from pleased. He glowered at the sea of serious
faces before him. The children had shuffled wearily into the
school hall and attempted the hymn half-heartedly, in a sing-
song sort of dirge and mumbled their way through the prayer.
They now stood, or rather slouched, as the deputy
headteacher scowled at them.

"Do you know, you have about as much energy this
morning as a cage of dead parrots," he told them. He
clapped his hands together loudly. "Stand up straight, and
look as if you are alive at the very least!"

Royston wondered how many cages of dead parrots
Mr Draycott had seen in his life. Not many I bet, he thought
to himself.

Mr Draycott shook his head dramatically and sighed.

"You wander into the hall like a lot of zombies, moan and groan your way through a hymn that is supposed to be about the joys of life, and say the prayer like a flock of lazy sheep with laryngitis!"

Mr Draycott is very fond of using similes, thought Royston, smiling to himself.

The class had been learning about similes - when one thing is compared to another - in English with Mrs Gabbitas, and Royston considered himself something of a star when it came to this area of the curriculum. Royston had been very pleased with his efforts, but Mrs Gabbitas had been less impressed.

"I think you are going rather over the top here, Royston," she had told him as she scrutinised his dramatic adventure story about pirates.

Mrs Gabbitas had screwed up her face as if she had been sucking a lemon, when she had read about 'the blood pumping out of the man's neck like crimson oil from a gushing oil well', and the 'eyeballs bouncing down the deck like two slimy tennis balls', and the 'sailor shinning up the mast like a squirrel with its tail on fire'. But Royston had thought they were rather good himself.

Mr Draycott was still rambling on.

"Is it any wonder, I say, is it any wonder at all, that we do so abysmally at sports?"

Royston did not think that the deputy headteacher was expecting an answer.

"Well is it? Look at you! You are lazy, apathetic, lethargic and about as fit as a herd of legless donkeys. All your get-up-and-go has got-up-and-gone! Too much television, too much sitting on your backsides playing on the computer and not enough exercise, that's your problem."

Isn't that three problems, thought Royston and what else would we sit on, if not our backsides?

"Last season we were bottom of the Inter-school Football League, bottom in the junior cricket, we gave a very poor showing at the Primary School Athletics Gala and we couldn't even rustle up a team for the mini-rugby competition. Now, let me tell you …"

"Excuse me, Mr Draycott."

All heads turned in the direction of the speaker. It was Mrs Gabbitas, who was standing by the piano. Like the deputy headteacher, she also looked far from pleased.

"I would just like to point out, if I may, that it is the boys who have been so unsuccessful in the sports. The girls have, in fact, done rather well. We were runners-up in the inter-schools rounders, a very creditable third in the netball, held our own in the hockey and Penelope Pringle, Gillian

Kershaw, Naseema Pervez and Noleen Midgley all returned from the swimming gala with medals and certificates."

"Yes, yes, that's quite true, Mrs Gabbitas," said Mr Draycott, clearly irritated by the interruption. "I am very grateful to you for pointing that out to me."

He clearly was not, thought Royston.

"I was, of course, speaking about the football, cricket and rugby. The girls have indeed done very well. It is just a pity that the boys in this school have not put in as much enthusiasm and energy as they have clearly done. Anyway, we are going to have the hymn and the prayer again, and I want to hear you raise the roof with your singing. I want to hear every word of the prayer delivered clearly, with gusto and as if you mean what you are saying. And if it is not a whole lot better this time, then we will remain in the hall and continue to do it until I am satisfied. Now, stand up straight, heads back, chins up, deep breaths and if you are ready on the piano, Mrs Gabbitas…"

"He really lost his cool this morning, and no mistake," said Simon Morgan to his mates as they made their way home after school that afternoon. "I've not seen him like that before."

"I have," murmured Royston. "Lots of times."

"That's because you're never out of his room, or Mr Masterson's," said Rajvir Singh.

"It's stress, you know," announced Fozzy. "He's suffering from stress. My dad was telling my mum about it last night. He's got stress, my dad. Had it for ages. He moans about work, moans about the neighbours, moans about my bedroom, moans about the weather, moans about the state

82

of the country. In fact he moans about almost everything.
He's never in a good mood these days. Snaps at me and my
sister, gets really angry about silly little things. He's always
complaining."

"Bit like you really, Fozzy," Royston remarked.

Fozzy decided to ignore the comment.

"He's no fun my dad, these days. Stress, that's what it
is. All grown ups get it as they get older. They look back to
when they were young and had lots of fun, don't like their
job any more and see their lives disappearing before them."

"Shut up, Fozzy! You're really depressing us," cried
Simon, punching his arm.

"I'm just explaining what's wrong with Mr Draycott!"

"Mr Gomersall doesn't get stress," announced Royston,
"and he's dead old. He's always happy and never moans,
and he's got more than most to complain about."

"Here we go again," groaned Fozzy. "Him and his
wonderful old-age pensioner."

"Well, I'm right," said Royston. "Mr Gomersall hasn't
got much money, lives by himself, can't move much because
of his gammy leg and he's just come out of hospital again,
but he's always cheerful. You never hear him complaining.

He says you've got to look on the bright side of life and make the best of what you've got."

"Well, I'm sick of hearing about the remarkable Mr Gomersall," said Fozzy. "All I'm saying is that Mr Draycott is suffering from the same thing as my dad."

"I never see my dad," said Simon Morgan sadly, "so I don't know whether he has stress or not."

That put an end to the conversation, and the three boys walked on home without another word.

On Monday morning, Mrs Gabbitas was in a particularly good mood.

"Well, I must say that the stories you wrote for me last week were most imaginative and full of lively words and interesting phrases. I read them all over the weekend and I was very pleased. Some of you have really tried to use some colourful similes." She looked in Royston's direction before continuing. "Perhaps a little too colourful at times, but nonetheless, I was very impressed by the effort you have all put in."

The classroom door creaked open and Mr Draycott entered, a gloomy expression on his face.

"May I have a word, Mrs Gabbitas?" he asked morosely.

"I was just telling the children what a lovely batch of stories I received on Friday, Mr Draycott," Mrs Gabbitas told him cheerily. "And how very pleased I am with their efforts."

"Really?" he replied, without a trace of a smile.

"I can see a definite improvement in their writing this term," the teacher continued brightly.

"Let's hope we will see a definite improvement in their
efforts on the sports field as well."

Mrs Gabbitas sighed heavily.

"So what was it you wanted, Mr Draycott?"

"Pardon?"

"What did you want to speak to the children about?"

"Oh, yes. Everyone look this way for a moment and sit
up at your desks. You look half asleep. I shall be having the
first practice for the football team this Thursday after school
and I want a really good turn out. I shall be selecting the
new side at the same time. I have also decided that we will
train after school every Thursday, and every Friday lunchtime thereafter, to get us all in shape. I do not want to be
bottom of the league for the third year running. If we all put
in the effort and attend the practices regularly, perhaps we
will do rather better in the sporting fixtures this season."

"Sir, it's my trumpet lesson on Thursdays, Sir,"

announced Rajvir Singh.

"And I've got my paper round, Sir," said Fozzy.

"We always go to the supermarket on a Thursday," said Simon.

"Sir, I can't …" began Timothy Joseph.

"You see! You see!" exploded Mr Draycott, turning to face Mrs Gabbitas, before swivelling around to scowl at the class. "This is what I am talking about! Where's the dedication? Where's the application? Where's the enthusiasm?"

The children returned his stare with blank faces, knowing full well that he was not expecting an answer. Then, Mr Draycott slumped on the corner of the teacher's desk and smiled. It was not a very pleasant smile.

"Perhaps you might like to tell me a more convenient time - an afternoon after school which will not interfere with your trumpet lessons, or your paper rounds, or your shopping trips, or whatever else you have on - when you will be able do me the great honour of gracing me with your presence?"

"I can do Tuesdays, Sir," said Ravir meekly.

"And I can too, Sir," added Fozzy.

"Tuesday's a good day for me, as well," said Timothy quietly.

"Right then. Tuesday it is. Tomorrow after school, you will appear kitted out and ready to be put through your paces. And I do not want any feeble excuses. Do you hear?"

"Yes, Sir," chorused the children.

With a flourish Mr Draycott swept out of the room.

"Stress," pronounced Fozzy, to no-one in particular.

The next afternoon after school, the boys were waiting on the field for the arrival of Mr Draycott.

"I hope I don't have to do much running about, jumping up and down or kicking," complained Fozzy. "I've got a verucca the size of Mount Vesuvius on my heel, festering athlete's foot, and an enormous in-growing toenail as well. My mum said I shouldn't overdo physical activity with feet like mine."

"How do you propose to play football, Fozzy," asked Timothy Joseph, "if you don't run about, jump up and down or kick? That's what football players do."

"He could go in goal," said Micky Lincoln. "There's not much running about, jumping up and down or kicking in goal."

"'Course there is!" cried Royston. "He's got to run to catch the ball, jump up to stop it going in the net and then boot it upfield."

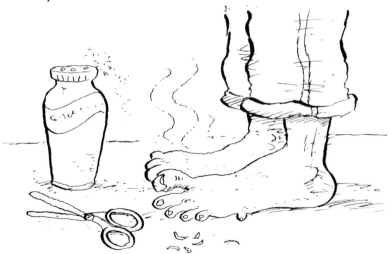

"Well I can't run about, jump up and down or kick and that's the end of it," retorted Fozzy. "My feet are a walking nightmare."

"Well, what are you here for then," asked Rajvir, "if you can't play football?"

"If you must know, I've only come this afternoon because I'd get it in the neck from the deputy headmonster. I know Devil-man Draycott. He'd make me stand up in assembly and go on and on about people like me being lazy and apathetic and lethargic, and all those other long words he uses. I am prepared to suffer any discomfort rather than face Draycott in assembly tomorrow."

"Did I hear someone mention my name, James Foster?"

The deputy headteacher had crept up silently behind the knot of boys. He was dressed in shiny funereal black shirt and shorts, thick black knee length stockings and huge black boots with white laces. A silver whistle dangled from his neck on a blood-red ribbon. Mr Draycott looked even more threatening in his football kit, with his great hairy legs like tree trunks, tufty black beard and arms like a gorilla's.

"Er... I was just wondering where you were, Sir," replied Fozzy feebly.

"Well, wonder no more, James," said the teacher, bending down to whisper in his ear. "I am here now and looking forward to putting you through your paces."

Fozzy felt it would not be appropriate at that moment in time to mention his volcanic verucca, his festering athlete's foot and the enormous in-growing toenail.

"Oh, great," he mumbled, trying to look keen.

"You boys should be running around the field," Mr Draycott told them, jogging up and down on the spot. "Passing the ball, dribbling, heading, getting in shape, not standing around like a group of old ladies waiting for a bus to take them on a seaside outing! Come along, do a circuit of the field and look lively." He rasped his whistle and the boys galloped off.

Mr Draycott watched them depart before joining Mrs Gabbitas and three girls who were watching from the sidelines. The girls were dressed in their rounders kit.

"I didn't know you had a rounders practice this afternoon, Mrs Gabbitas," remarked the deputy head, without taking his eyes off the line of runners that had now slowed down to a snail's pace.

"There isn't a rounders practice, Mr Draycott," she told him.

"Well, we welcome all the support we can get," said the deputy head. He shook his head and blew on his whistle sharply. "Just look at that sorry shower limping its way around the field. Get moving you boys, speed up!"

"The girls are here for the football trial," said Mrs Gabbitas. "They want to play football."

Mr Draycott's mouth dropped open and his whistle fell out.

"Girls!" he exclaimed. "Playing football?"

"That's right," replied Mrs Gabbitas.

He gave her a patronising look and then chuckled to himself.

"I hardly think that the rough and tumble of a football match is the sort of things girls would enjoy, Mrs Gabbitas."

"You mean they would be better off at home playing with their dolls, Mr Draycott?"

"Mrs Gabbitas ..."

"My girls are very good athletes, and what is more they are very keen to play football. Aren't you, girls?"

"Yes, Miss," chorused the three figures.

"And I don't suppose there is anything in the school football league rules which prevents girls from playing?"

The deputy headteacher smiled uncomfortably.

"Well I'm sure it is very commendable of you girls to show willing, but football is a boys' game. It's a rough, tough, dangerous business. People can get hurt. I would suggest you stick to rounders, netball and hockey."

"Girls play football, Sir," piped up Penelope Pringle. "My cousin Prudence plays and she's at the high school."

Mr Draycott scratched his head and struggled to find the right words.

"That's... er... really very interesting, Penelope, but I think your parents would have something to say if I started including their daughter in a potentially dangerous contact sport like football."

"They wouldn't mind," Penelope replied. "I told them I was coming for the practice and they were very pleased."

"Were they really?" mumbled Mr Draycott.

"My mum and dad wouldn't mind either," said Naseema Pervez. "I play football with my brothers. I have done since I was little, and I go with them to matches on Saturday."

"My dad's a referee," added Gillian Kershaw, "so I know all the rules."

Mr Draycott had stopped listening and was watching a very sorry group of boys pant and puff and hobble their way back to where he stood, with his hands on his hips and a face like thunder.

"That was pathetic!" he exclaimed, when the red-faced, wheezing band of boys collapsed in a heap on the grass beneath him. "Can't you even run around the field without ending up like a herd of exhausted carthorses? And where is James Foster?"

"He's having a bit of a rest, Sir," Rajvir told the deputy headteacher, gasping and pointing to the fence at the far side of the field where Fozzy was sitting, legs stretched before him. "He's got problems with his feet, Sir."

"He'll have more than problems with his feet when I get hold of him!" cried Mr Draycott.

"So what about it then?" asked Mrs Gabbitas.

"What about what?" asked the deputy head.

"About the girls playing football?"

Every one of the boys sat up sharply, like puppets that had had their strings yanked.

"Girls!" they shrieked in unison. "Playing footy!"

"Don't look so surprised," said Mrs Gabbitas calmly. "I bet they can show you boys a thing or two." She turned to Penelope, Naseema and Gillian. "Why don't you show Mr Draycott and these boys how to run around a field?" she continued smugly. "Off you go."

The girls shot off like hares and loped their way around the field in no time at all. They sprinted back to Mrs Gabbitas with an exhausted Fozzy Foster limping at the rear. Then they stood with expectant faces looking at the astonished deputy head.

"Well?" said Mrs Gabbitas, smiling.

"Well..." repeated Mr Draycott.

"Can we play then, Sir?" asked Penelope.

"It's not quite as simple as that," explained Mr Draycott loftily. "I concede that you girls can run and pretty quickly as well, but how would you shape up in a match when faced with rough boys?"

"Well let's see, shall we?" said Mrs Gabbitas. "Come on girls. On the pitch."

"Well, I've seen everything now," moaned Fozzy in disgust as the boys trudged home later that afternoon after the football practice. "Girls playing football! Girls! I ask you."

"They were good," murmured Simon sadly. "They were very good."

"They were," agreed Rajvir, aiming a stone at the gutter and missing by miles.

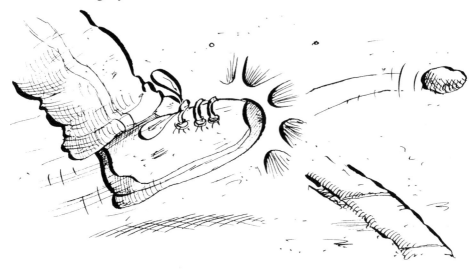

"They were lucky, that's what," said Royston. "The only reason Naseema managed to get past me was because I momentarily lost my concentration."

"And what about Gillian taking the ball off you all the time?" asked Timothy.

"Twinkletoes?" snapped Royston, pulling a gruesome face. "Huh. She's light on her feet and can dance about a bit because she does ballet. Anyway, I didn't want to tackle her hard because I could have hurt her and then I'd have been in trouble for being too rough."

"Admit it, Royston," said Simon. "They were better than us. A lot better. They could dribble better, had better ball control, they passed better, headed better and were more accurate kickers. They were better. Admit it."

"They were," agreed Rajvir.

"Girls," moaned Fozzy. "What is the world coming to when girls play football?"

The first match of the season was against Cornfield School. Mr Draycott's heart had sunk when he saw the first fixture. Cornfield had won the cup the previous year and had been top of the league for as long as anyone could remember.

"Well, that's it," the deputy head told Mrs Gabbitas. "We haven't a cat in hell's chance of beating them."

"Don't be so pessimistic, Mr Draycott," Mrs Gabbitas chided him. "The practices have gone really well and the children have turned up every Tuesday and Thursday, rain or shine. Even if we don't beat Cornfield we will certainly win other games and we won't end up bottom of the league again."

"That's true, I suppose," said the teacher, brightening up a little. "I have to admit they have trained hard."

It was a wet, cold, drizzly Saturday morning when the first match of the season was played. The Cornfield School team sprinted out onto the pitch like professional footballers

in their pristine white football strips, with the school logo - an ear of corn, in bright yellow - displayed proudly on their chests. They began their warm-up exercises, heading the ball skilfully, bobbing, passing, dribbling, dodging, weaving and jumping. Then the Bogglesview team appeared. It was a motley assortment that jogged onto the field. Some were in red tops, others in blue, Fozzy was in irridescent orange and Royston was in a T-shirt that had seen far better days. Some had white shorts, others black. Fozzy's shorts were long and scarlet. The three girls were dressed identically in green strip.

"Dear oh dear," sighed Mr Draycott as he stood with Mrs Gabbitas on the touch line. "This is going to be so embarrassing. Of all the teams to play first, we have the bad luck to be playing Cornfield. And look at our lot. They're like the remnants of a jumble sale. And you-know-who'll be over in a minute smiling and flashing his teeth like a hungry shark."

"Who?" asked Mrs Gabbitas.

"Old 'Smiler' Simmonite, headteacher of Cornfield, gloating away, showing a mouth full of teeth as usual."

"Come on, Mr Draycott," replied Mrs Gabbitas. "Cheer up and sound a bit more enthusiastic."

Mrs Gabbitas was wrapped up in a shapeless grey duffel coat, thick woollen skirt and bright knitted bobble cap with matching gloves. A multicoloured scarf twisted itself around her neck like some strange exotic snake. She reached into her capacious shopping bag and produced a large thermos flask.

"Would you care for a cup of coffee to warm you up?"

"No, no thank you, Mrs Gabbitas," replied Mr Draycott

gloomily. "I'm quite warm enough. In fact, I'm a bit hot under the collar, if truth be known." He suddenly craned his neck and looked out across the pitch. "You see that big gangly boy?" he said solemnly, pointing to a tall, dark, wiry lad with wild, woolly hair. "The one who looks like a stick insect. Well, he plays for the county juniors. He's like greased lightning when he gets the ball. I remember him from last year."

"He looks about sixteen," observed Mrs Gabbitas, putting the flask back in her bag.

"He's the Cornfield captain and he's like a dynamo."

The player in question headed the football deftly into the air, bounced it off his head a few times and then let it slide slowly down his long body and onto his instep. He bobbed it backwards and forwards from one foot to the other before propelling it with incredible force into the empty goal.

"We haven't got a chance," groaned Mr Draycott.

The headteacher of Cornfield School sidled up, a self-satisfied smile playing on his thin lips. He was a small, sharp-faced man with a thatch of sandy hair, eyes like shiny blackcurrants and ears like jug handles. He rather resembled a cunning ferret.

"Good morning," he said breezily, rubbing his long hands together vigorously. "Not the best of days is it? A trifle cold and wet, but fresh."

"Morning," mouthed Mr Draycott, as his voice was whipped away by the wind.

"Having said that," continued Mr Simmonite, "we play really well in these conditions."

"Wonderful," murmured Mr Draycott.

"And your team?"

"Yes?" Mr Draycott turned to face him. "What about my team?"

"A rather colourful assortment of strips," remarked the headteacher, smirking.

"It's not what they are wearing," replied Mr Draycott. "It's how they play that matters."

"Yes, yes of course," replied his grinning companion. "And I suppose it's not really economic to buy new school football shirts and shorts for your players."

"What do you mean?" asked Mrs Gabbitas suddenly, pulling the woolly python from her face.

"Well, football strips are so expensive and of course, if they are rarely used it seems rather a waste of money to splash out on them."

"Like you have done," retorted Mrs Gabbitas.

"Are you a parent?" asked the headteacher of Cornfield

School, rather taken aback by the aggressive woman in grey, who was now staring at him with a look that would kill at a hundred paces.

"No," replied Mrs Gabbitas. "I'm the teacher of these children and assistant team coach. I suppose from that comment about football strips you are implying that we will be knocked out early in the competition."

Mr Simmonite chuckled and gave her a sympathetic smile.

"You were last year."

"Yes, well this is this year and we have a set of new players on the team," she told him icily.

"Girls? I can see you have some girls in the team." Mr Simmonite raised a sandy eyebrow and did his imitation of a shark again.

"We are very big on equal opportunities at Bogglesview," Mrs Gabbitas told him. "Aren't we, Mr Draycott?"

"Oh, yes," he replied wearily. "Very big."

As the teachers were talking, the whistle blew and they turned their attention to the pitch. The game had begun.

Cornfield kicked off and the ball went straight to the tall, dark, wiry boy. He booted it straight ahead and shot after it, leaving Simon panting behind him. Royston raced up the field, but by this time the boy had side-stepped Rajvir, manoeuvred his way around a startled Micky Lincoln and lined himself up for a shot at the goal. Fozzy stared at him with eyes like saucers. But just at that moment, Gillian Kershaw appeared out of nowhere and, with a beautifully balletic move, tiptoed the ball from between the tall boy's feet and back-heeled it down the field. The boy stopped dead in his tracks, hardly believing that the ball was not there any more.

However, Cornfield soon got possession again and two of their players belted up the field towards a frightened Fozzy, who stood like a luminous totem pole in the middle of the goal mouth. Simon, Royston and Timothy Joseph descended on the Cornfield player who had possession, a small ginger-headed boy with an explosion of freckles on his face. He was nifty and quick, and cleverly dribbled around them. He was moving into a better position to have a shot at goal when in stepped Gillian again and tapped it to Simon, who kicked it downfield. Rajvir chased after it, but two Cornfield players loomed towards him and soon the captain of their side had possession again and was striding towards Fozzy. This time he was too fast and with a powerful kick banged it into the corner of the net. One-nil to Cornfield and a cheer went up from their many supporters on the touch line.

"Good goal!" shouted the headteacher of Cornfield School.

"Let's finish the job!" shouted the captain as he galloped down the pitch, revelling in all the patting and hugging and hand-shaking from his team mates.

The first half was not quite as disastrous as Mr Draycott had predicted. Cornfield were certainly having to put in a great deal of effort. True, every time a Bogglesview player got the ball it was plucked from them. True, each time Fozzy kicked the ball upfield it was collected by a player on the opposing side and returned to their half, but Mr Draycott was very pleased when the Bogglesview team gathered around him at half-time.

"You are doing very well," he said.

"Very well indeed," echoed Mrs Gabbitas.

"We're 1 - 0 down though," said Royston.

"Just remember, Royston," said Mrs Gabbitas, "they are the best team in the league and it's not as if they are having an easy ride."

"Certainly not," agreed Mr Draycott.

Mr Draycott was about to give the team a pep talk, but Mrs Gabbitas was quicker off the mark.

"Now look," she said firmly, "we are doing well and you are putting in the effort, but we are supposed to be a team here, working together to win, so it is no earthly good kicking the ball when you get hold of it and then rushing upfield after it. You need to pass it to somebody in a better position. That's what the other side are doing. For example, every time you get the ball, Royston, you hang on to it like a bulldog with a bone, instead of using your head and passing it to somebody better placed to score. Penelope was in prime position on several occasions, but you hung on to the ball and then lost it."

Mrs Gabbitas seems to know an awful lot about football, thought Royston.

"It's that tall lad with the wiry hair, Miss," said Micky. "He's faster than a greyhound after a rabbit."

Mrs Gabbitas smiled. That lesson on similes was certainly bearing fruit.

"He is very fast," conceded Mr Draycott, getting a word in at last.

"I know he's fast," agreed Mrs Gabbitas. "Everyone can see that, and it's no earthly use high-tailing it after him when he's shooting off down the pitch. He needs marking. So, Rajvir, why don't you just stay with him and get between him and the ball, and him and the goal? That can be your job. Stick to him like glue. The rest of you boys pass the ball around. Simon, you've just been standing there like a tailor's dummy, waiting for one of the girls to pass it to you on a plate. And don't hog the ball. Pass it back if you see someone in a better position to have a go at the goal. Did you want to say anything Mr Draycott?" she asked, turning to the deputy head.

"No, nothing," he replied. "I think you've said it all."

In the second half, Royston kicked off. He passed it to Penelope, who side-footed to Simon, who immediately lobbed it forward to Gillian. Three big players from the opposing team lunged towards her, but Gillian danced around them undeterred, flipped the ball into the air and passed to Royston who had found a space. Royston could not believe his luck. There was a clear opening. He belted the ball, and

fell to his knees as he watched it soar into the air and
plummet in a great arc through the goalie's outstretched
hands, landing with a thud in the back of the net.

The Bogglesview players went wild. Simon performed
a perfect somersault, Rajvir waved his arms wildly above his
head, and Fozzy, who had evidently forgotten about his
poorly feet, stomped out of the goal and began to dance a jig
for the benefit of the startled spectators. Mr Draycott leapt in
the air before grabbing an astounded Mrs Gabbitas and
giving her an enormous hug.

"Mr Draycott!" she exclaimed. "Really!"

"We've scored! We've scored!" he yelled. "We've
scored a goal!"

The headteacher of Cornfield school was no longer
doing his imitation of a great white shark, but was looking on
in bemused silence.

The goal had given the Bogglesview team a great deal
more confidence and had wiped the smug smiles off the faces

of the players on the opposing side. They were taking the Bogglesview team in their multicoloured outfits much more seriously now.

Rajvir shadowed the captain of the Cornfield team as instructed, Royston and Simon passed the ball more, Timothy and Micky seemed to have discovered new reserves of energy, and raced up and down the field like rabbits. Then as the game was nearing the end, something quite miraculous happened. The Cornfield team were getting increasingly fed up at having to chase the ball backwards and forwards, so when Naseema got possession and hesitated for a moment, they surged forward. Quick as a flash, Naseema flicked the ball to Micky. Micky immediately passed to Royston, who suddenly saw an opening. He was about to have a shot at goal when he saw Penelope waiting in space, in a much better position. He whacked it towards her. Penelope received the ball, tipped it back with her right foot and shot to the left. The ball soared high into the air, travelling in slow motion through the cold autumn air. The Bogglesview team held their breath. Where would the ball land? The goal keeper leapt high to his right. He got his fingers to the ball, but lost his balance and the ball plummeted to the ground, rolling slowly into the back of the net.

Mr Draycott and Mrs Gabbitas looked stunned. They stood on the side lines stock still, mouths open, like fish out of water, watching the Bogglesview team leaping and shrieking for all they were worth.

"Are my eyes deceiving me, Mrs Gabbitas," he whispered, "or did we score again?"

"We did indeed," she replied. "We did indeed."

However, the elation did not last long. Cornfield's frustration had increased and the players started to get more aggressive in their tackling. Simon received a vicious kick to the ankle and responded by pushing the offender onto the ground - in the penalty area.

"Penalty!" shouted the referee.

"Penalty?" screamed Simon. "No way."

"Do you wish to leave the field, young man?" asked the referee calmly, taking out his little black book.

"No," said Simon weakly. "Sorry."

The referee replaced his notebook.

"Penalty!" he roared.

Everyone knew who would take it.

The tall, wiry boy with the frizzy hair placed the ball carefully on the penalty spot and stared menacingly at Fozzy, who stood in the goal trying hard not to look like a frightened rabbit. Fozzy had decided that the best thing to do when faced with superboy was to get out of the way of the ball as quickly as possible. There was no way he could stop it. It would be like trying to catch a cannonball. Fozzy watched the Cornfield captain position himself and bit his bottom lip nervously. There was a deathly silence. Mrs Gabbitas gripped Mr Draycott's arm. The headteacher of Cornfield School looked as though he was frozen to the spot. But then, another miracle occurred. The ball flew through the air at phenomenal speed. Fozzy leapt out of the way, but landed badly on his verruca. With a cry of pain he shot back in the opposite direction. The ball hit him with a sickening thud on the side of his head and ricocheted clear of the net.

Fozzy felt the world go dim with the sound of whooping and cheering, and the distant whistling that signalled the end of the match, ringing in his ears.

It was all over.

Mr Draycott stared at the sea of smiling faces before him. It was the first junior assembly of the week and he looked very pleased, very pleased indeed. The football team swaggered into the hall and stood straight-backed and bright-eyed as the deputy head grinned widely at them.

"Do you know," he chortled. "I am the proudest deputy headteacher in the world this morning. I am as pleased as a dog with two tails, because on Saturday the football team scored an historic victory, a victory which will go down in the history of Bogglesview school, a victory which will be talked about for many years to come..."

"You know a lot about football, Miss," Simon said to Mrs Gabbitas later that morning.

"Yes I do, Simon, don't I?"

"Why, Miss?"

"Well, because I played football when I was younger, that's why."

"You did, Miss?" exclaimed Fozzy.

"I was captain of the women's soccer team at college."

"You were, Miss?" exclaimed Fozzy again.

"And I was a pretty good player, even if I say so myself."

"Wow!" cried Micky Lincoln.

"I played in goal. Of course football wasn't my best game."

"Was it hockey, Miss?" asked Penelope.

"No."

"Netball, Miss?" asked Naseema.

"No, not netball either," replied the teacher.

"Rounders, Miss," suggested Gillian.

The Christmas Play

"Come on everybody!" Mrs Gabbitas shouted enthusiastically, as a meandering stream of pupils entered the hall after school. "Liven up!"

It was the first meeting for the Christmas play. The previous year, lots of children had taken part in the pantomime. It had been great fun and a huge success, but this year the wave of interest had dwindled to a mere trickle of really keen pupils. That was because Mrs Gabbitas had chosen to put on a Nativity Play. She had decided that a bit of gentle persuasion was in order and had dragooned most of her class into taking part.

"Miss, that's what little kids do!" protested Fozzy Foster when he heard. "We did them nativity plays in the Infants!"

"Not like this one, Jamie," explained Mrs Gabbitas. "We are going to perform a medieval Miracle Play, a biblical pageant dating back many hundreds of years. It's extremely entertaining and will be absolutely super on stage."

The only pupils happy with their parts were Timothy Joseph, Christopher Wilkinson and Noleen Midgley (The Three Wise Men) and Penelope Pringle, who had been given the main part of Mary.

"Can I be a king, Miss?" pleaded Fozzy. "Please!"

"No, you can't, Jamie," replied Mrs Gabbitas. "There were only three kings and I've picked the people for those parts."

"I'd be brilliant as a king."

"I've cast you in another role, Jamie. It's a very demanding part and ideal for you."

"It's not a camel is it?"

"No, it's not a camel."

"Or a palm tree. I was a palm tree in the infants and I got terrible cramp. I can't stand still for long."

"It's not a palm tree, either," the teacher told him.

"Please let me be a king, Miss," pleaded Fozzy.

"No!" snapped the teacher.

"But how can Noleen Midgley be a king, Miss?" persisted Fozzy. "She's a girl."

"That has not escaped my notice, Jamie," replied Mrs Gabbitas, smiling at her own wit. "We live in an age of equal opportunities," she went on to explain. "I think it only fair that we should give the girls a fair crack of the whip. Don't you?"

"First football," complained Fozzy, scowling dramatically, "and then they take over Christmas!"

When he found out the 'very demanding part' that was 'ideal' for him was the part of the Archangel Gabriel, he was far from pleased.

"I'm too big for a start," he told his pals on the way home that afternoon. "I'll look really gormless with a pair of daft wings, dressed in a white sheet with tinsel round the bottom and a halo on my head." Nobody disagreed. "And fancy casting Noleen Midgley as a king. First they play football, then they're given boys' parts in the play. Girls!" Nobody disagreed with that either.

"What about me?" complained Simon Morgan, "I'm cast as the First Shepherd. I don't even like sheep - they scare me silly - and wool brings me out in a big red rash anyway."

"I might as well not be in it," Micky Lincoln joined in morosely. "The Innkeeper only has a few words to say."

"You can swap with me then," said Royston Knapper, equally down-in-the-dumps. "I've been picked for Joseph, which means I'll be holding Penelope Pringle's sweaty hand for half an hour."

"You might have to kiss her as well," gloated Fozzy, delighting in someone else's misfortune. "I'd sooner play the Archangel Gabriel in my underpants in front of a packed hall, than have to kiss Penelope Pringle. EEEEErrrrrhhhhhh!"

Royston and Penelope, started rehearsals by glaring at each other over the crib and arguing over who should hold the big plastic doll representing the Baby Jesus.

"You have Him for a bit!" Penelope grumbled. "He's getting heavy!"

"I'm not holding a doll!" Royston replied indignantly, pushing it back.

"Go on," insisted Penelope, thrusting the doll into Royston's hands.

"I said no!" he shouted.

"Well, I say yes!"

"Nooo!"

Mrs Gabbitas entered the hall to see Mary and Joseph propelling the plastic doll backwards and forwards like a rather violent version of 'Pass the Parcel'.

"Don't drop the Son of God!" she bellowed.

After a few weeks of rehearsals, things improved and Royston, though he would never admit it, found that he quite liked acting alongside Penelope. All the moaners stopped complaining and began to enjoy themselves. They actually looked forward to putting on the play.

It was the day before the performance and Mrs Gabbitas, dressed very festively in green dungarees, and bedecked in colourful silver jewellery like a Christmas tree, gathered the cast around her for a final bit of advice.

"Now, children!" she said, showing a mouthful of teeth like piano keys. "Tomorrow we go on stage in front of mums and dads, and some very important guests. The Mayor and Mayoress will be there, the vicar, Reverend Windthrush, Mr Craddock the school inspector, and a reporter from the paper. So, I want it to be really good. Remember my little motto: 'We do the play the Gabbitas way!' That means: Firstly, no snifflers and snufflers on stage. Some of you have colds, so before the show - have a blow. I don't want a cast sounding like a herd of anteaters with sinus trouble. Secondly, no chewers and chompers. All chewing gum, bubbly, sweets, crisps and the like, must be got rid of before going on stage. Put them in the rubbish bin. There will be a large bin offstage for that purpose. Thirdly, no bumblers and mumblers. Speak clearly, slowly and loudly and look at the audience. And remember it's 'Away in a Manger', Michael Lincoln, not 'A Wayne in a Manger.' Now, is everyone clear what to do?"

"Yes, Miss," chorused the cast.

"Splendid!" Mrs Gabbitas smiled widely. "I'm sure it will be a great success."

Unfortunately, Mrs Gabbitas changed her mind less than five minutes after the curtain opened on the very first evening. The play started well. Penelope, dressed in blue and looking pretty and shy, was excellent, and Royston made a very sympathetic and confident Joseph. It was with the arrival of the Archangel Gabriel that things started to go badly wrong.

Rather than making a serene and angelic entrance, the Archangel collapsed onto the stage, crushing a wing and bending his halo in the process. Concentrating as he was on keeping his halo straight and manoeuvring his wings around the set, Fozzy trod on the bottom of his long white costume, forgot about the rubbish bin offstage and fell flat on his face. Eventually, he clambered to his feet, adjusted his halo and straightened his wings. Then, he opened his mouth:

"Oh gentle maiden, dressed in blue, *sniff*,
I come from God with news for you, *sniff*,
With heavenly tidings of great joy, *sniff*,
You are to have a baby boy, *sniff*.
This joyful news I gladly bring, *sniff*,
And He will be the King of Kings, *sniff*, *sniff*.

"Blow your nose, Jamie! Blow your nose!" repeated Mrs Gabbitas in a loud whisper from the wings.

Hearing her voice offstage made Fozzy's mind go completely blank. He froze. Then he sniffed.

"Jamie! Give your nose a blow! Give your nose a blow!" Mrs Gabbitas whispered again loudly.

Penelope stepped in cleverly to help him out.

"And angel, what else should I know?"

"She said to give my nose a blow," replied Fozzy.

"What?" Penelope cried.

"I mean, The Son of God will come to Earth
And all will celebrate his birth."

Mrs Gabbitas raised her eyes heavenwards. What more could go wrong? She had not long to wait.

Onto the stage strode the first of the Wise Men -

Timothy Joseph. His grandma had really gone to town on
the costume. He was shrouded in a long red velvet cape with
silver stars and wore a great golden crown which had slipped
down his forehead. He carried a large box under his arm but,
to Mrs Gabbitas's horror, was chewing away merrily on a
gigantic piece of pink bubblegum.

> I have travelled from afar,
> *chomp, chomp,*
> Following the distant star,
> *chomp, chomp,*
> Through wind and rain and snow and sleet,
> *chomp, chomp.*
> I've come to worship at His feet,
> *chomp, chomp,*
> For he's the King of Kings, I'm told,
> *chomp, chomp,*
> So I have brought this gift of gold,
> *chomp, chomp.*

Mrs Gabbitas greeted him furiously when he eventually appeared offstage.

"Does no one listen to what I say?" she said in an angry whisper. "Where's the bin?"

"Pardon, Miss?" asked Timothy.

"I said, where's the bin?"

"Miss, I've bin on stage," he replied.

Mrs Gabbitas struggled to keep herself calm.

"Timothy, I did not say: 'Where have you been?' I said: 'Where is the bin?' - the rubbish bin, so that you can remove the gum you have been chewing for the last five minutes."

"Oh heck," said Timothy quietly. "I forgot, Miss, sorry."

Then Simon Morgan, First Shepherd, entered.

The weather, it is really cold,
scratch, scratch, scratch,
My sheep are frozen in the fold,
scratch, scratch, scratch,
My legs and hands and feet are chapped,
scratch, scratch, scratch,
It is a long while since I napped,
scratch, scratch, scratch.

Mrs Gabbitas covered her face with her hands.

There was one pupil who did not forget what Mrs Gabbitas had said. Micky Lincoln's mum, dad, grandma, grandad, Uncle Michael and Auntie Christine, and assorted cousins and relations were all out front, and he was determined to make his few words memorable. He meant to do exactly as Mrs Gabbitas had said: speak clearly, slowly and loudly.

When Joseph knocked on the inn door to ask if there was room inside, Micky strode out aggressively.

"What?" he demanded.

"Have you any room, Innkeeper?" asked Royston politely.

"No!" replied Micky loudly. "Clear off!"

"You must have some room," continued Royston.

"We haven't!"

"But your inn is large and there are only two of us."

"Tough luck!" growled Micky, really getting into the part now, and adding to his few lines as the mood took him. "There's no room - so on your bike!"

Royston did not remember these words, but carried on with his next line.

"I've got my wife out here on the ass," said Royston, "and she's having a baby."

118

"So what?" grunted Micky. "It's nothing to do with me."

Mrs Gabbitas felt a tight knot in her stomach, and her heart began thumping in her chest. 'Disastrous! Disastrous!' she mouthed to herself.

Behind the scenery, as the children took their bows, cheerful Mrs Gabbitas - the loud, the happy, the colourful - was transformed into tearful Mrs Gabbitas - the silent, the pallid and the cold.

Nevertheless, despite all the catastrophic events of the play, Mrs Gabbitas heard a loud and enthusiastic audience clapping and cheering, and she felt slightly better. Then she saw Mr Masterson approaching her and the feelings of dread returned.

"Mrs Gabbitas," said the headteacher, "I wonder, would you mind coming down to my room for a moment, please? There are one or two things I would like to say."

Mrs Gabbitas' mouth went horribly dry and beads of sweat started to form on her brow. By the time she arrived at Mr Masterson's room, she was a dribbling wreck! What on earth were they going to say to her? She had tried her very best and failed them all.

As she opened the door of the headmaster's room she was greeted by the Mayor, Councillor Armistead, a big, round man with a red face and fat fingers. The other important guests present stopped talking as she entered the room.

"Well," said the Mayor. "I've seen some nativity plays in my time, but I've never, ever seen one like that."

Mrs Gabbitas's eyes filled with tears.

119

"If I could explain…" she began, but was interrupted.

The Mayor continued, "I've seen nativities in infant and junior schools, in comprehensives and colleges, but I've never seen one like that!" He paused. "It was grand, absolutely splendid! The children loved it and so did the audience. My sides were sore with laughing and the last part brought tears to my eyes! It was magnificent. I'm sure that Reverend Windthrush will agree," - he turned in the direction of the vicar - "when I say that that's how nativity plays should be presented. Ordinary people, speaking plain language, bringing the Christmas Story to life as it happened hundreds of years ago. Well done Mrs Gabbitas!" he said, and shook her hand warmly.

"Yes, indeed," echoed the vicar. "A very impressive production. Most good-humoured and thoroughly enjoyable. Not a dry eye in the house."

"The children did splendidly," remarked Mr Craddock, the school inspector. "Well done, Mrs Gabbitas. A truly memorable evening."

And while Mrs Gabbitas, glowing with pleasure, listened to the praises and the compliments of the important guests and told them of her plans for the next production, two of the cast crunched through the crisp snow on their way home.

The sky was the darkest blue, speckled with tiny silver stars, and the smell of pine was in the air. Christmas trees winked and twinkled with lights from front rooms, and the cold, winter moon shone down. It was the magic atmosphere of Christmas.

One figure coughed quietly, then spoke.

"You were ever so good."

The other figure replied.

"You weren't so bad yourself."

"Happy Christmas, Penelope," said Royston Knapper, slipping his warm hand around her cold fingers.

"You weren't *that* good, Royston," said Penelope, gently removing her hand and shoving it deep into her pocket. "See you tomorrow, and put that mistletoe away."

"Yeah, see you tomorrow," mumbled Royston.

And the two, red-faced friends trudged happily home.